"This is what turns me on—"

The pressure of his mouth on hers became insistently persuasive. That Jason was an expert lover, Eden was in no doubt. He seemed to draw the very soul from her body with the intimacy of his kiss.

At last he released her, stepping back to survey her flushed cheeks. "Yes," he murmured, "that's what turns me on."

She didn't need to be told that. His desire had been evident. She put up a hand to her tousled hair, aware it had been Jason's hands holding her head immovable for his kiss that had caused the disorder.

"You're disgusting!" she snapped. "How dare you kiss me like that when you're going to marry another woman?"

He raised dark eyebrows as he questioned, "I am?"

CAROLE MORTIMER
is also the author of these

Harlequin Presents

Many of these titles are available at your local bookseller.

For a free catalogue listing all available Harlequin Romances and Harlequin Presents, send your name and address to:

HARLEQUIN READER SERVICE,
M.P.O. Box 707, Niagara Falls, NY 14302
Canadian address: Stratford, Ontario N5A 6W2

CAROLE MORTIMER

ice in his veins

Harlequin Books

TORONTO • LONDON • LOS ANGELES • AMSTERDAM
SYDNEY • HAMBURG • PARIS • STOCKHOLM • ATHENS • TOKYO

Harlequin Presents edition published June 1981
ISBN 0-373-10437-5

Original hardcover edition published in 1981
by Mills & Boon Limited

CHAPTER ONE

EDEN KNEW THERE WAS SOMETHING WRONG as soon as she joined her mother and stepfather for drinks before dinner; knew it by the tightness around her mother's painted mouth and the way her stepfather kept trying to soothe her. Poor Drew—he didn't have an easy time of it with his fiery wife.

She accepted the martini he held out to her, smiling in gratitude as she waited for the explanation of her mother's upset. Something was definitely wrong with her; Eden had never seen her so upset.

"Where were you all afternoon?" her mother demanded to know.

"I was at Cheryl's playing records," she replied dazedly. "Why?"

"Because you had a visitor, that's why."

"Anyone interesting?" She sipped her drink.

"Anyone interesting!" Angela repeated shrilly. "Of course it was someone interesting, or I wouldn't be in this state."

Eden frowned at her mother's agitation. "Who was it?"

"Jason Earle!"

"Jason Earle? But I don't know any Jason Earle."

"The newspaperman," Drew put in before his wife exploded.

"*That* Jason Earle...." She whistled through her teeth. To say he was a newspaperman was an understatement. He was one of the most powerful men in the world, controlling a vast portion of the media. "And you say he came here to see me?"

"Yes. And he looked down his haughty nose at me with his steely gray eyes, ripping me to pieces at a glance!" The ice rattled in the glass as Angela's hand trembled with anger. "He was so damned arrogant!"

"Calm down, Angela," Drew advised. "There's no point in working yourself up about this."

"No point—"

"Why on earth should he want to see me?" Eden interrupted her mother's tirade. "I don't know the man."

"We haven't seen any of them since Eden was two years old, and now David has decided—"

Eden looked startled. "What does my grandfather have to do with Jason Earle's being here?"

"Everything!" Angela paced the room in her agitation. "After eighteen years he's decided he would like to see you again, and he's sent that man over here to try to talk you into it. He says he's a friend of David's, but I'm sure he's been going out with Isobel the past few years."

Isobel, Eden knew, was her father's second wife. She knew the history of her parents' broken marriage, knew that Graham Morton had been engaged to marry Isobel Dean until he had met and fallen in love with her mother, and that within a few weeks of meeting her parents had married each other, much to the disgust of Graham's father, David Morton.

David Morton had done everything in his power to break up the marriage, wanting his son to marry the daughter of his old friend Russell Dean. He had undermined Angela at every turn, ridiculed her until she could take no more and had issued her husband an ultimatum: his father or her. Graham had chosen his father, and had married his former fiancée after his divorce.

Eden had been two years old at the time of the breakup, and only three when her mother had married Drew. Consequently she had always considered him to be her father, and his family her own. It seemed incredible to her that her real father's family should suddenly take an interest in her after all this time; that her grandfather should want to actually see her.

"Perhaps Jason Earle *has* been seeing Isobel," Drew acknowledged. "But he's here for David Morton, not her."

"Oh, I know that," Angela said scornfully "Isobel and I never had any time for each other. She always made it clear that she would take my husband from me the first chance she had."

"That's past history now," Drew said quietly. "It's the here and now we have to concern ourselves with. David has sent this Jason Earle to see us because he would like to meet his granddaughter."

"Then he should have come himself; it would have made more sense than to send a stranger," his wife snapped.

"He's an old man, Angela, well into his seventies."

"He would never have come himself no matter what age he is," she said disgustedly. "He wanted to get rid of me so that Graham could marry Isobel, and he had no interest in us once he had managed to get Eden and me out of his life. Of course, he had no way of knowing that Graham and Isobel wouldn't give him any more grandchildren," she added with satisfaction. "That Eden would be the only true relative he has now that Graham had died. But I won't allow Eden to go, Drew. I won't allow it!"

Eden frowned. "Won't allow me to go where?"

"To England, of course," her mother snapped irritably. "Haven't you been listening to anything I've said?"

"Well, yes, but—"

Suzy, the maid, came in at that moment. "Mr. Earle is here, Mrs. Shaw," she informed her employer.

"Well, show him in," Angela said abruptly, waiting until the young girl had left the room before speaking again. "Now you, Drew—" she hurriedly straightened his tie "—you are not to let him daunt you."

He gave a short laugh. "I have no intention of letting him—"

"You haven't met him," Angela interrupted, standing back to survey her husband critically. She turned her attention to Eden. "And don't let him force you into agreeing to anything. We have to talk this over as a family."

Eden was curious to meet this man who had put her mother into such a fluster. It wasn't easily done, so he must be quite something.

"Mr. Earle." Suzy gave a shy smile before disappearing.

Eden's first impression was of a tall lithe man, the focal point being a pair of steely gray eyes that flickered over them all with cool disdain. He wasn't merely handsome; that was too weak a description. He was striking, breathtakingly attractive. Eden was struck dumb by the vitality, the magnetism, he emitted.

He was like no one she had ever seen before, had ever expected to meet. The black dinner suit he wore was tailored to his powerful frame, his linen immaculate. He was in his mid-thirties, she guessed, with a muscular physique that showed no signs of excess flesh, a look of cynicism in his eyes, a hardness in his mouth that should have detracted from his attractiveness but seemed only to make him more so.

She was no longer surprised by her mother's antagonism; after Drew's easygoing nature, this forceful man must be something of a shock to her. She could see that Drew was slightly overwhelmed by the other man, despite his assertion that he wouldn't be. Thank goodness she was looking her best, since she intended to go to a disco later with Tim. She knew the black velvet cat suit suited her slender curves, that it made her hair even more golden than usual, made the short cap look like spun gold as it framed her smooth cheeks, giving depth to her golden eyes and color to her creamy skin.

The man she knew as Jason Earle shook hands with her stepfather, but for all the notice he took of her she might as well not have been in the room.

He was talking to her mother now. "I expected your daughter to be here," he said curtly.

Her mother gasped, "Eden—"

"Yes—Eden." He said her name as if he had difficulty in getting it off his tongue. "I expected the child to be here."

Child! At twenty that was something Eden didn't consider herself to be. She stepped forward into the light, the smile freezing on her lips as those icy gray eyes swept over her with barely concealed insolence. This man might be devastatingly attractive, but his manners left a lot to be desired.

She took a deep breath, meeting that critical gaze unflinchingly. "I am Eden," she told him in a slightly husky voice, her American accent only slight, as it had never been encouraged by her mother.

He looked momentarily taken aback before the cold mask was back in place. "You are David Morton's granddaughter?"

He gave Eden the impression that he now expected her to deny it. "My name is Eden Shaw, but I believe David Morton is my grandfather," she told him distantly.

His irritation was obvious. "I expected you to be... younger."

"Really?" She raised her eyebrows. "My grandfather

probably thinks of me as a child. I was two the last time he saw me," she added dryly. "When you get older you have a way of trying to forget the passing of the years. I'm sure you know that yourself." She knew this last was insulting, but this man's condescending attitude was not something she was prepared to accept.

He showed by the narrowing of those icy gray eyes that her insult had not gone unnoticed, and by the look on his face it wouldn't go unpunished, either. "I'm sure David knows exactly how old you are; he never forgets anything. But now that I have seen you for myself I feel I've had a wasted journey "

"Probably " She gave a toss of her head.

"Shall we go into dinner?" Angela suggested tersely. "We can talk about this later."

"Unfortunately I can't stay to dinner," their guest refused, not looking sorry about it at all. "I came only to arrange to take your daughter back to England with me on Monday. I have people to meet for dinner this evening, business acquaintances."

"I see," Angela said tightly, angered by his obvious snub. "Then we won't keep you," she dismissed him.

"About Monday—"

Eden, too, was aware of his deliberate show of a desire to avoid their company. He must have known they would assume by his dress that he would be dining with them. God, he was an arrogant swine!

"As you've already realized, Mr. Earle," she interrupted, "I'm old enough to take myself to England if I had any desire to go there. But I don't, and I have no intention of going to England on Monday or at any other time. England has never appealed to me," she drawled insolently. "And even less so now. I hear one can die of the cold over there without anyone being aware of it," she added tauntingly, hoping her double meaning wouldn't be lost on him.

Those cold gray eyes raked over her mercilessly, narrowed and speculative. "I believe that the winters over here can be even more severe," he snapped tersely.

Eden raised one blond eyebrow. "Were we talking about the season...?"

There was a dangerous tension about him now, an aura of anger barely kept in check. "Perhaps not." He glanced at his wristwatch. "But I don't have the time right now to persuade you that it would be in your best interests to visit your grandfather."

Her harsh laugh rang out. "If you're talking about monetary gain, Mr. Earle, you can forget it. The last thing I've every needed from David Morton is money."

His look was chilling. "Perhaps tomorrow would be a better time to discuss this."

"Are you sure you can spare the time?" she asked sweetly. "You appear to be rather busy," she added by way of explanation, although she knew he was as aware as she was that that hadn't been her meaning at all.

His mouth tightened. "No, I don't have the time." He appeared unworried by her gasp at his honesty. "So perhaps you wouldn't mind meeting me at my hotel for lunch."

Eden didn't want to meet him again at all, let alone in the privacy of his hotel. "I don't—"

His mouth curled contemptuously. "I didn't mean in my suite," he mocked, "but in the dining room of the hotel. I don't think either of us has any desire to be alone with the other."

"I'm afraid it's out of the question, Mr. Earle," Angela cut in. "We make it a rule always to have Sunday lunch together. It's the one English tradition I refuse to give up."

"I see," he said thoughtfully. "Then perhaps dinner would be more convenient?" He looked straight at Eden.

She was unnerved by the directness of that gaze. She wished her mother had invited him to lunch tomorrow, although in the circumstances it was perhaps understandable that she hadn't. "I, er—"

"Would eight o'clock suit you?" He took her hesitation for agreement to his suggestion.

"I . . . yes, I suppose so."

"Good." He nodded his satisfaction with the arrangement. "I'll call for you here."

"Wouldn't it be easier for me to meet you at your hotel?"

"Perhaps," he agreed curtly. "But I would prefer to call for you. People might misunderstand the situation."

That brought a smile to Eden's lips, her golden eyes dancing with mischief. "Meaning you wouldn't like the management to think you have young girls calling for you," she taunted.

"Quite," he acknowledged tersely.

Her grin deepened. "Very well, Mr. Earle."

He looked at her parents. "I trust you have no objections to my talking to your daughter?"

"No—"

"None at all," Angela interrupted her husband. "As long as you do only talk. Any decision that is made about Eden's visiting David will obviously have to be a family one."

Jason nodded. "I can understand that. Now if you will all excuse me . . . ."

Angela rang for the maid to show him out, keeping a tight-lipped silence until she was sure he was out of earshot. "The nerve of the man!" she finally burst out. "The sheer nerve of the man!"

Drew wordlessly handed her a drink, watching her take a large swallow of it before he thought it safe to speak. "Not a man to oppose," he remarked softly. "I should think he's broken people and not given a damn what happened to them. A man who likes to be in control—at all times."

His wife's blue eyes flashed angrily. "I didn't ask for a breakdown of the man's character—or an assessment of his sexual prowess."

"Mummy!" Eden gasped.

Drew frowned at his wife. "That wasn't what I meant, and you know it."

"I suppose not," she grudgingly agreed. "Although remembering Isobel, I don't think you would be far wrong. I shouldn't think she has a lot to offer in that direction. All right, all right," she sighed at the censure in their faces. "Forget I said that. But you do see why he annoyed me so much when he came by this afternoon."

"Oh, definitely," Eden said forcibly. "I thought he was horrible."

"And you, Drew?" his wife inquired. "What did you think of him?"

He seemed to consider for a moment. "I thought he was...interesting."

"Interesting!" she echoed scornfully. "What sort of an answer is that?"

He shrugged. "I wouldn't like to pass an opinion on him. On the surface he's everything you said he was, but underneath—who knows? Jason Earle appears to me rather like an iceberg, ninety percent of him below the surface."

"You mean that arrogance was only ten percent of him?" gasped Eden.

Drew laughed at her expression. "Maybe twenty," he conceded.

She shivered. "I hate to think what the other eighty percent is like."

"I doubt if anyone knows that. He didn't seem the type

to let anyone even know what he's thinking, let alone get close to him."

"Oh, don't let's talk about him anymore," Angela dismissed the subject. "He's already ruined my lunch today; I have no intention of letting him do the same thing with my dinner."

Despite her mother's dismissal of the man, Eden was aware of a tension among them as they ate their meal. She felt sure their thoughts were all running along similar lines— her grandfather's sudden wish to see her after all these years of silence. She had forgotten she had any other family than her mother and Drew, had even taken Drew's surname for her own. She knew her real father had died when she was five years old; driving too fast on a slippery road, he had skidded straight into a tree and been killed instantly. As her mother had pointed out, his second marriage had produced no children, hence her grandfather's interest in her now.

She had to admit to a certain amount of curiosity about her family in England, a sneaky longing at the back of her mind to know exactly what sort of man her grandfather was. Her father must have been very weak to have been ruled by him as he had been, which suggested that her grandfather's nature was as forcible as their visitor's. No wonder the two men were friends!

And yet her grandfather hadn't made one inquiry about her in eighteen years, had never even bothered to ascertain whether she was alive or dead. To turn around now and ask to see her, to expect her to drop everything and rush over to England, seemed to her to be the height of arrogance. Besides, didn't her father's second wife still live in the same house as David Morton? And Jason Earle was the last person to send to persuade her to take that flight; everything about him had antagonized her.

No, she had already told him she wouldn't go, and she meant it. Nothing he said to her tomorrow or at any other time would make any difference to her decision.

SHE WAS WAITING IN THE LOUNGE when Tim arrived for their date that evening, putting down the magazine she had been flicking through to move into his arms for his kiss. He was two years older than she, and they had been dating for the past six weeks. Not very long, really, but longer than most of her relationships lasted. Perhaps it was because she spent so much time in her stepfather's company, but most of the boys she dated seemed childish after a while, always trying to get her into an intimate relationship and finishing with her when they realized she had no intention of sleeping with them.

Tim was different—rich, self-assured, and very sophisticated for his age. She enjoyed his company immensely, found his light lovemaking pleasant, and hoped he felt the same way about her.

She laughingly smoothed away some of her peach lipstick from his mouth. "Must remove the evidence," she teased.

Tall and athletic, with tanned skin, sun-bleached blond hair and the deepest blue eyes she had ever seen, Tim was every girl's dream. He smiled down at her, that heart-melting smile that never failed to win the women over. Even her mother fell for it, approving of him wholeheartedly.

He placed his lips on hers again. "Mmm," he sighed against her parted mouth. "I don't give a damn who knows I've been kissing you."

Eden snuggled against him. "Neither do I."

"Where are your parents tonight?"

"Gone to the Merricks' for the evening." She moved unhurriedly out of his arms.

"Hey," he teased, flicking a curling tendril of hair away from her face. "I'm not about to attack you just because we're alone here."

She grinned at him, pulling on her short white woolly jacket. "I know you aren't." Their lovemaking had never gone beyond a passionate kiss and a tentative caress.

Tim frowned. "I'm not sure I like that, this natural assumption you have that I wouldn't even try."

She arched an eyebrow at him. "And would you?"

"I might," he said slowly. "If I didn't know three servants would come running at the first cry of rape."

She watched him through lowered lashes. "I'm not about to cry rape."

"You aren't?" His blue eyes quickened with interest.

"No." She opened the door. "I'm about to go outside to your car!" And she laughingly left the room.

Tim caught up with her outside, opening the door of the low sports car for her before getting in beside her. He turned to look at her in the darkness, the snow lying around them outside like a white carpet. "You were teasing me in there, weren't you?"

Her golden eyes challenged him as she snuggled down into her jacket. "Was I?" she asked throatily.

He sighed, switching on the ignition to maneuver the car out into the steady flow of traffic. "Yes, you were."

She looked at him closely, noting a certain tension about his mouth. "Are you angry with me?"

He sighed again, turning to give her a warm smile. "No, Eden, I'm not angry with you. But I wish you wouldn't play with me. One of these days I'm going to take your teasing seriously."

"You mean...."

"Yes, I mean! I know you're an innocent, Eden, but I'm not. It can be quite a strain behaving like a gentleman. Not that I mind," he added hastily. "But it doesn't help when you keep playing with me."

"I never realized...." She looked at him with new eyes, seeing him not as the fun-loving partner of innocence of the past six weeks but as the young rich socialite that he was. Seeing him like this, she could well imagine that there had been plenty of girls in his life who would give anything to become the wife of Tim Channing, heir to millions. It was something she had never thought about before, shedding on him a new light. And she wasn't sure she liked it.

"You aren't that innocent, Eden," he scorned.

She blushed in the darkness, glad he couldn't see her confusion. "I didn't mean that," she said impatiently. "I meant that I didn't realize about...about...."

"The girls in my past," he finished for her. "You grow up quickly in the society I mix with."

She knew he was sophisticated for his age, had admired the way he always took control on their dates together, but it had never occurred to her that his relationships with other girls hadn't been as innocent as their own friendship. Somehow this new knowledge frightened her, unnerved her, made her suddenly shy with him.

It made her wonder if their mutual friends thought their relationship more intimate than it actually was. Color flooded her cheeks at the thought. She couldn't bear people to think such things about her, no matter how erroneous those thoughts were.

She looked down at her clenched hands. "I suppose so," she mumbled.

Tim gave her a sharp look. "Hey, are you okay?"

She gave him a quick nervous smile, looking hurriedly away from his probing glance. "I'm fine," she lied.

One of his hands left the steering wheel to cover the nervous movements of hers as she fidgeted with her small black evening bag. "I've shocked you, haven't I?" he guessed with a sigh.

She attempted a light laugh, flicking her head back in a careless gesture. "Don't be silly, Tim. I'm not a child who doesn't know the facts of life."

"No, but you are an innocent, no matter how assured you like to act. I'm sorry; I didn't mean to upset you."

"I'm not upset." Her attempt to laugh it off sounded dismal even to her own ears.

"Shocked, then."

"I'm not that, either," she lied. "Good heavens, Tim, this is the twentieth century, and you're quite old enough to do what you want, with whom you want."

"Yes, but—"

"Let's drop the subject, Tim," she said sharply, uncertain in her own mind of why she was so shocked by his disclosure. She was aware that most of her friends freely engaged in sexual relations with their boyfriends. Why should Tim be any different from them, especially with the temptations he must have had? She was being stupid, childish, all the things he accused her of being, and yet she couldn't stop herself. "Where are we going tonight?" She herself changed the subject.

"Delanie's. Claire will be meeting us there later. She and her date are having dinner elsewhere." Claire was Tim's older sister, a hardheaded career woman who had sacrificed any idea of marriage to her job as editor of a popular women's magazine. She had little time for men, and Eden was surprised at her having a date this evening. Not that Claire Channing wasn't beautiful—she was, extremely so—but her intelligence and ambition often frightened away any would-be boyfriends. Besides, few men liked to date a woman who was earning more money than they were.

"I didn't realize she had a boyfriend." Eden couldn't hide her curiosity.

Tim grinned. "She doesn't. This is an old friend, someone she's known for years. Whenever he's in town she drops everything to go out with him."

He must be something to affect the supremely confident and hardened Claire in this way. Eden felt a burning curiosity about the man who could make Claire forget her job. She herself liked Claire, had tremendous respect for her, but given the same choice, a career or marriage, Eden felt sure she would choose quite differently. But then, Claire was nothing like her.

"Have I ever met him?" she asked now.

He shook his head. "It must be six months since he was last here. But don't worry, you'll like him; most women do. Although I don't want you to like him too much," he added hurriedly. "And don't be bowled over by his charm."

"Is that likely?"

"Oh, yes."

Eden could feel herself starting to relax, the tension leaving her body. She laughed huskily, back on a footing with Tim she could cope with. "Could I make you jealous, Tim?" she teased.

"All too easily. Although I wouldn't recommend it tonight: Claire is likely to do you an injury if you attempt to steal him away from her!"

"She likes him that much?"

"And the rest. She would marry him tomorrow if he asked her."

"And will he?" So there *was* someone Claire considered more important than her career!

"Not in a million years," Tim said with brutal honesty.

"Does Claire know that?"

"Oh, sure. But where he's concerned she isn't too proud to accept any crumbs he cares to give her!"

"You mean...."

Tim laughed softly at her expression. "Poor Eden, this is your night for shocks. Yes, I mean they're lovers."

"And yet it's six months since she last saw him?" She was dumbfounded.

He nodded. "But it could be six years and she would still go running when he snapped his fingers."

It didn't sound like the Claire she knew, the Claire who could handle the advances of any man with chilling hauteur. "Doesn't it bother you?"

"Why should it bother me? Claire is a big girl; she makes her own decisions."

"Yes, but—"

"I'm not her keeper, Eden. If she chooses to make a fool of herself every time the guy comes to town, that's up to her. She wouldn't thank me for interfering."

Eden could well imagine she wouldn't! "Perhaps not, but—"

"Wait until you've met him, Eden, and see for yourself how she changes in his company. No one could fight that."

"You like this man, don't you," she stated with certainty, noting a certain respect when he spoke of the other man.

"Sure, I like him." He parked the car, turning in his seat to look at her. "Have you been put off the Channing family by these blunt revelations? Has it shocked you too much?"

She was a little less sure of her feelings toward him, but she wasn't about to admit that to him, to show her naiveté any more clearly than she already had. She smiled brightly. "Of course not."

He caressed one of her creamy cheeks with long gentle fingers. "I'm glad about that, because I do care for you,

Eden, more than for any other girl I've ever dated. I wouldn't like to think I had frightened you off me."

He had a little, but she wouldn't tell him that. "I'm not easily frightened," she said jokingly. "Now, shall we go in?"

Tim straightened in his seat before getting out to come around and open the car door for her. He wrapped her jacket more firmly around her by pulling the lapels close together, bending to kiss her lightly on the nose. "Don't go away," he ordered huskily, moving to lock the car before coming back to her, his arm around her shoulders as he held her to his side. "I wish Claire weren't joining us now; we could have ducked out and gone somewhere to be alone."

"With what in mind?" Her golden eyes were guarded.

"Now, Eden," he rebuked gently. "Haven't I always behaved perfectly with you?"

"Perfectly," she agreed.

"And I'm not going to behave any differently now. I respect and like you too much. Okay?"

"Thank you." She smiled at him shyly.

"Mmm, now forget the conversation we had in the car. I'm a nice guy, remember?"

"I remember," she laughed.

And she did try to keep that thought in mind during the next hour, tried to get back on the mildly flirtatious footing they had always been on. But something had changed between them, bringing a new awareness that hadn't been in their relationship before. She did her best to hide her uncertainty with him, joining in his lighthearted bantering with a gaiety she hoped only she knew was forced.

His admission of experience shouldn't have had this effect on her; she had been out with other young men who she knew had an equal experience. And yet she was becom-

ing very fond of Tim, more than fond, and she didn't like
to think there had been other girls in his life who had
shared an intimate knowledge with him.

She felt a certain amount of relief, therefore, when he
announced the arrival of his sister and her escort. He stood
up. "Try not to show your disapproval," he bent down to
whisper in her ear.

"Oh, I wouldn't!" she told him indignantly.

He grinned down at her. "I know it."

She acknowledged his teasing with a smile before turning
to look at the approaching couple. What she saw made her
gasp, and her face went pale. Pushing her way through the
crowds of people was Tim's sister, Claire, looking breathtakingly beautiful as usual, her long sun-bleached blond
hair waving glowingly down her back, her perfect face alight
with pleasure, the deep red halter-necked dress she wore
molded to her slender curves.

But it wasn't Tim's sister who made her gasp; it was her
escort. Looking arrogantly confident, his hand resting
lightly on Claire's elbow as he guided her toward their table,
was Jason Earle! And by the look on his face as he recognized Eden, he was no more pleased to see her there than
she was him.

CHAPTER TWO

EDEN STARED AT HIM with openmouthed amazement. Not because he had lied when he said he had a business dinner; she couldn't give a damn about that. Rather, she was amazed because of what Tim had said about his sister and this man. If what Tim had said was true—and she had no reason to doubt it—then the fact that Jason Earle was also seeing Isobel Morton put no restrictions on him at all.

The two men were shaking hands. "Good to see you again, Jason." Tim's pleasure in meeting the other man again was obvious.

"Tim." Jason Earle nodded his greeting.

"Let me introduce you to Eden," Tim said with pride. "Eden, this is Jason Earle. Jason, my girl friend, Eden Shaw."

"Miss Shaw." Jason Earle's handshake was very formal, although the mocking inquiry in those steely gray eyes was not.

"Mr. Earle," she returned equally formally.

Claire sat down in the chair Jason pulled out for her, smiling good humoredly. "I hope you two are going to drop this 'Mr.' and 'Miss' bit." she laughed. "'Eden' and 'Jason' would be so much more friendly."

Eden was well aware of that, which was why she intended to continue calling him Mr. Earle. She had no wish to be friendly with him now or at any other time. How could he turn up here with Claire when, according to her

mother, he was supposed to be marrying Isobel Morton?
Didn't he care if the other woman found out about Claire?
Obviously not, if his behavior in meeting Claire openly
was any indication. He was probably as sure of Isobel Morton's feelings toward him as he was of Claire's.

He sat between Claire and herself, very much the man in
control as he ordered drinks for them all. He turned to
Claire. "Miss Shaw and I are not friends, and so unless she
asks me to I couldn't possibly call her by her first name."

"Oh, don't be so chilling, Jason." Claire glowed up at
him, looking much younger than her thirty years. "Forget
your stiff English manners for once."

He smiled at her. "It isn't a question of my stiff English
manners," he told her smoothly. "Miss Shaw may prefer
me to be formal." He turned to look at her, those cold gray
eyes seeming to read her thoughts.

"Eden doesn't mind, do you, honey?" Tim put in.

Her eyes flashed with dislike as those steely gray eyes
continued to look at her. Jason Earle had deliberately put
her in this position, his veiled mockery telling her he knew
exactly what her little game was. She looked away from him
with a tightening of her mouth, sipping her drink before
answering. "No, I don't mind," she finally said. "Why
should I?"

Jason Earle bowed his head in mock acknowledgement.
"Thank you—Eden."

She gave him a brittle smile. "That's perfectly all right—
Jason."

"Good, that's settled, then." Claire sat back more com-
fortably in her seat, her hand reaching out to entwine with
Jason's. "We've just had a lovely meal, haven't we, darling."

"It was…enjoyable," he agreed.

Claire laughed. "How you English love to understate

things! But perhaps it wasn't the meal that was so enjoyable; perhaps it was the company."

"You flatter me, my dear."

Eden looked away, sickened by the adoration Claire made no effort to hide. It probably wouldn't have been so bad if Claire weren't normally such a levelheaded person, but for her to be so captivated by this man seemed completely out of character. And Jason Earle accepted her adoration as his due, played with her emotions like a master fiddler.

Eden's contempt for the man grew as the evening progressed, and a couple of times she actually had to bite her tongue to stop herself from being openly rude to him. She stood up with a certain amount of relief when Tim once again asked her to dance.

Jason Earle stood up, too. "Would you mind if I had this dance with Eden?" His request was directed at Tim.

Tim raised surprised eyebrows, giving his sister a quick look. He shrugged. "I suppose not. Eden?"

She drew a ragged breath, her annoyance deepening at the challenge she could read in Jason Earle's expression. "I have no objection," she accepted coolly.

He guided her to a space on the dance floor, pulling her into his arms to move slowly to the rhythm of the music. The top of her head on a level with his chin, Eden was very aware of the tangy smell of his after-shave and the less tangible smell of his body, a completely male smell that wasn't unpleasant—in fact, the opposite.

The group on the stage was one she particularly liked, the music soft and romantic, and she had to stop herself from relaxing against the taut hardness of this man's body, to resist the temptation to yield to the arms clasped around her waist. She had been surprised by the way he had made no effort to dance more formally, holding her lightly to him, his warm breath softly fanning the hair at her temple.

The tension between them was unmistakable, and finally Eden could stand it no longer, throwing back her head to look at him. "Your business dinner turned out to be more enjoyable than you had anticipated," she said sarcastically.

"Not at all," he returned smoothly, meeting her gaze unflinchingly. "I always enjoy my dinners with Claire."

Her mouth turned back sneeringly. "So Tim has been telling me."

He smiled, a completely natural smile that made her breath catch in her throat. He really was a most attractive individual, and perhaps Claire's infatuation with him wasn't so difficult to accept after all. "I'm sure he has," he acknowledged softly.

Eden looked away from that smiling mouth, determined not to be affected by the charm he could display when he chose to. "You really had no need to lie about your dinner date being a business one," she told him. "We didn't particularly want you to stay anyway."

Jason laughed softly. "Leash your claws, little girl," he advised softly. "My dinner with Claire was exactly what I said it was—business."

"Oh, yes?" she scorned, her golden eyes disbelieving.

"Yes," he nodded. "Claire works for me."

Her eyes widened. "For you?"

"I own the magazine she runs."

"Oh!" She couldn't deny that this information had taken her by surprise, but really she ought to have made the connection herself. "I see. But would Isobel Morton see your...dinner in the same light?" she inquired sweetly.

His mouth tightened into a thin line. "Meaning?"

"Oh, I'm sure you know what I mean, Mr. Earle."

"No, you tell me."

She shrugged. "It's public knowledge that you're going to marry my father's widow."

"Is it now?" he queried softly.

"Oh, yes. Do you think she would approve of your seeing Claire?"

"Do you intend telling her?"

"Me?" She couldn't hide her surprise. "Why should I tell her? I've never met her and already I dislike her. She broke up my parents' marriage, she and my grandfather. Besides, it's nothing to do with me."

"I couldn't agree more," he said grimly, his arms tightening painfully around her waist and so pulling her closer to the hard strength of his body. "I consider my private life none of your business."

"But you do intend marrying Isobel Morton?" She wished he would let her go. The music had changed twice since they had come onto the dance floor, and she could see Tim giving them anxious looks. And as for Claire...!

"I may be," he agreed tightly.

"Does Claire know about that?"

He raised dark eyebrows. "Are you by any chance threatening me?"

Eden opened wide innocent eyes. "Threatening you? I have no idea what you mean, Mr. Earle."

"Oh, I think you do, Eden." His voice was icy. "I don't react well to threats."

Her laugh wasn't quite as confident as she would have liked it to be. "I think you have misunderstood me, Mr. Earle. I merely wondered if Claire knew you were shortly to be married."

"I'm well aware of what you wondered," he snapped. "And although I may have been a friend of Isobel's for some time now, there have been no wedding plans made, no matter what may or may not be public knowledge," he added mockingly. "Tell me, why didn't you just come right out and tell Tim and Claire that you know me?"

"Why didn't you?"

He shrugged. "I took my cue from you. You didn't seem to want them to know."

"I didn't see the point, as I have no intention of going to see my grandfather. But don't worry, Mr. Earle, I won't tell Claire about your other . . . friend."

"Claire knows about Isobel," he told her coldly. "I've never made her any promises concerning our own relationship."

"I don't suppose you need to; the poor woman worships you," she said disgustedly. "I find it quite nauseating to watch."

"Then don't," he advised abruptly.

"It's a little hard not to." She moved out of his arms. "Shall we go back to the table, Mr. Earle, now that you have assured yourself that I don't intend making things awkward for you."

"You can make things as awkward as you want, Eden— or attempt to. I don't think Claire would be particularly bothered by anything you have to say. But I do think we should return to the table. We've said all we want to say to each other—for the moment."

"Does that mean I can be excused from having dinner with you tomorrow?"

Jason's mouth thinned angrily. "You make it sound as if I forced you into the arrangement."

"And didn't you?" she challenged.

"I don't think so." He met that challenge unflinchingly. "I think you're under a misapprehension concerning this proposed visit to your grandfather. Quite frankly, I couldn't give a damn whether you go to England or not. I promised your grandfather that I would see you and suggest it to you, and as far as I'm concerned, I've done that."

"So you feel your obligation to my grandfather is fulfilled?"

"I'm not under any obligation to your grandfather. I was coming to New York on business and so I—"

"Decided to do an old man a favor," she finished.

"Yes." He took her arm and almost dragged her back to the table.

"I thought you were never coming back." Tim leaned forward to kiss her lightly on the nose as she sat down next to him.

She raised her face for his kiss, ignoring the mockery clearly visible in the watching gray eyes. "Mr. Earle thought it best to get all our duty dances over in one go," she said rudely, hitting out at the man who unnerved her with just a look.

Tim looked surprised by her outburst. "I—"

Eden laughed lightly at his expression. "Only teasing, Tim. Mr. Earle and I were talking and forgot the passing of the time."

"Yes." Jason relaxed back in his chair, his arm thrown casually across Claire's shoulders. "We were discussing the fact that Eden is David's granddaughter."

Claire frowned. "David Morton?"

"Mmm," he nodded.

"Then she's—"

"Graham Morton's child by his first marriage."

"I see," Claire said tightly.

Eden wished she did. She hadn't for one moment thought Jason Earle would blatantly admit to their knowing each other, although perhaps she should have realized what he would do: hadn't his eyes promised punishment earlier when she had been disparaging about his age? That Claire knew who David Morton—and consequently Isobel Morton—were was obvious, although Tim looked a little puzzled by the conversation.

"I don't understand." He looked at the two of them. "Did you know each other before today?"

"Not before today, no," Jason answered.

"How strange that you should meet through Tim and me," Claire said softly.

"But we didn't." Once again Jason answered for them both. "I called on Eden and her parents earlier this evening."

Claire's blue eyes passed calculatingly over the two of them, the dreamy glow she had had all evening slowly evaporating. "Why didn't you tell us that when Tim introduced you?"

Jason shrugged. "There was nothing to tell."

Tim still looked puzzled. "I still don't understand the relationship. I thought Drew was your father."

"Stepfather," Eden corrected him. "Don't look so surprised, Tim." She gave a light laugh. "Divorce and remarriage are quite common nowadays."

"But I...I didn't know. I always thought Drew—"

"He's the only father I've ever known or wanted," she said firmly. "I don't go around broadcasting the fact that my real father was a weak man who was ruled by his own father, that he—"

"That's enough, Eden," Jason cut in. "It isn't necessary to go into all the details of your parents' marriage breakdown."

"No! Because if I did that your precious Isobel might come under fire."

"I believe we've already dealt with my relationship to Isobel," he warned harshly.

"Well," Tim broke the awkward silence. "This is a. a...."

"Surprise?" Eden finished sweetly. "Yes, isn't it. Mr. Earle and I were quite bowled over by the surprise of it all. He was the last person I expected to see here this evening." Especially with Claire Channing.

"Let's dance, Jason," Claire suggested.

Eden studied the bottom of her glass until the other couple was safely away from the table. The last thing she had wanted was to have an argument with Jason Earle in front of the Channings, but he had put her in an awkward position by mentioning her grandfather, forcing her into explanations she would rather not have given, to Tim or to anyone else.

"Why didn't you tell me you knew Jason?" Tim hissed angrily. "I felt like a damned fool just now when he told us."

"How could I tell you? I didn't know he was Claire's mysterious lover."

"But later, when I introduced you," he insisted.

She slammed her glass down. "I was embarrassed, especially after what you had told me about Claire and him."

"Hell, yes! I'm sorry." He reached for her hand, smoothing his thumb over her skin. "I had no idea he was almost related to you."

Her head flicked back defiantly. "He isn't," she snapped. "Isobel Morton is no relation of mine. And I hardly know Jason Earle. He just called briefly on my parents earlier."

"But everyone knows Jason Earle."

"*Of* him," she corrected. "Can we leave, Tim?" She put a hand up to her temple. "I have a headache," she lied. "Besides, I'm not enjoying myself—not with *him* here."

"You should have explained to me earlier," he chided gently. "I know Jason is seeing Isobel Morton in England, and if you had just told me the connection . . . ." He shrugged. "I would have understood and got you out of here."

"Can we leave now?" she persisted.

"We'll make our excuses once they get back."

"They'll probably be relieved to see me go." She attempted a smile.

The smile faded from her lips as she looked up to meet taunting gray eyes. Her mouth tightened resentfully as she met that gaze defiantly, although it was finally her gaze that dropped and turned away. There was something about Jason Earle that tied her up in knots and brought out the worst in her. But she didn't know what it was.

Tim stood up. "I hope you don't mind if we leave now," he said with a smile. "Eden has a headache."

"Really?" Jason Earle obviously didn't believe this for one minute. "Then perhaps we should all leave."

"Oh, no—please," Eden protested sharply. "I don't want to break up your evening. Tim is just going to drive me home."

"Oh, do let's stay, Jason." Claire's hand rested lightly on his thigh as he sat next to her. "We have only this evening together. I think it's very mean of you to make a business appointment for tomorrow evening. No one works on a Sunday," she pouted.

Eden had looked at him sharply on hearing Claire's words. So Jason had told her he had a business meeting tomorrow evening, had he? Now was her chance to hit back at him for his earlier disclosure. And yet one look at his face told her that was exactly what he expected her to do. Well, she wouldn't give him that satisfaction!

"I understand you're here only for a couple of days, Mr. Earle?" she inquired politely.

He nodded distantly. "I leave Monday afternoon."

She raised her eyebrows. "So soon?"

"My business should be completed by then."

"But surely America has other...attractions?"

"Possibly."

Claire smiled up at him. "It holds me, doesn't it, darling," she purred. Her hard blue eyes flashed to Eden. "I'm sure Mrs. Morton would understand that I only borrow Jason occasionally."

"Would she?" Eden returned softly.

"Oh, I'm sure she would. I wouldn't mind in her position."

"No, I don't suppose you would." Eden didn't like clashing with Claire. They had nothing in common, but they were usually polite to each other. It was Jason Earle again, causing unnecessary friction. "And I really couldn't care whether Mrs. Morton would mind or not. I don't owe her any favors."

"Shall we go, honey?" Tim lightly touched her arm.

She gave him a bright smile. Poor Tim—he thought she was going to get into another argument. "Yes, let's. Good night, Claire, Mr. Earle."

"Until tomorrow, Eden," came Jason Earle's parting shot.

"Good night," she repeated hurriedly, taking hold of Tim's arm and pulling him away. She would meet Jason Earle for dinner tomorrow if only to tell him what she thought of him. He had taken malicious satisfaction in that last comment.

Tim hung back. "What did he mean by that?" he demanded to know. "Are you seeing him tomorrow?"

She sighed. "Wait until we get outside, Tim."

"But—"

"Outside, Tim," she pleaded.

He gave in reluctantly, and she could see he was very annoyed. She couldn't blame him for feeling that way, for she was angry herself.

"Now—" he turned to her in the warm confines of the car "—what did he mean?"

"I'm having dinner with him tomorrow."

"With Jason?"

She couldn't meet the accusation in his eyes. "Yes."

"But why?" he frowned. "You aren't dating him, too, are you?"

"Certainly not," she denied indignantly. "I would have thought it was obvious that I can't stand the man. He wants to talk to me about my grandfather, try to persuade me to go and see him."

"I see. I just didn't realize Drew was your stepfather."

Eden's mouth tightened, anger in her golden eyes. "As far as I'm concerned he's my father. My real father gave up any right he had to expect anything from me when he divorced my mother and married Isobel Dean. He made no effort to see me after his remarriage."

"Perhaps he thought you would be better off with your mother," he pointed out reasonably.

"Perhaps he did, and he was right. But that didn't mean he had to give me up completely. The agreement was that he had access to me anytime he wanted. I don't ever remember seeing him, *or* my grandfather."

"But surely—"

"There can be no excuse for what he did, Tim," she interrupted tightly. "And I despise my grandfather even more for the way he manipulated my father."

"I take it Jason is going to try to make you change your mind about seeing him?"

She shrugged. "He can try, although I don't think he'll bother. He's already told me he's doing this only as a favor to my grandfather."

Tim started the car, maneuvering out into the traffic. "You have to admit this evening was quite funny in a way." He gave a wry chuckle.

"I'm glad you think so!" She tried to sound angry, but somehow the humor of the situation reached her, too.

"You should have seen his face when he saw I was your date! Although I must say he recovered from it well."

"He must have done; I didn't notice anything was wrong."

"You wouldn't with a man like him." She sobered, her dislike back in full force.

Tim gave her a searching glance. "Why don't you like him? Is it because he's going to marry Isobel Morton?"

"If Isobel is anything like I think she is, then he deserves her," Eden snapped. "But I dislike him because he's arrogant, egotistical, superior in every way. He's just everything I despise in a man. His relationship with your sister while he intends marrying another woman is enough to prove what sort of man he is. I'm sorry, Tim, but I simply don't like him. He's too sure of himself and other people's reactions to him."

"Including your own?"

"My dislike doesn't bother him; in fact, he probably enjoys it. He enjoys tormenting me, anyway," she said with a grimace.

"Tormenting you?" Tim repeated sharply.

"Well, teasing me, then. Oh, let's not talk about him anymore, Tim. He depresses me."

"How's your headache?"

"Gone," she blushed.

"You didn't really have one, did you?"

"No," she admitted.

"I didn't think so."

"I don't suppose they thought I had one, either. But if I'd stayed there with him much longer I might have resorted to actually hitting the man." She shrugged. "What does it matter? They wanted to be alone, and so did we."

He smiled. "It doesn't matter to me. If I'm not going to see you tomorrow I'll have to make the most of tonight."

"I don't want to have dinner with him. I can't see the point of it when I've already made up my mind."

"I don't suppose it will hurt to listen to him."

"Probably not." she grinned. "I'll get a nice dinner out of him, anyway."

Tim halted the car outside her parents' house. "Can I come in for coffee?"

She got out onto the sidewalk. "You don't normally need to be asked."

"Great," he smiled, locking the car.

Eden moved around the kitchen preparing their coffee, the staff having finished for the day. Her mother and Drew weren't back yet, and so she and Tim had the house to themselves. Tim came into the kitchen just as she was placing the pot of coffee on the tray.

"What are you smiling at?" She frowned, puzzled, as he stood watching her with a silly grin on his face.

He leaned back against the refrigerator, his arms folded across his chest. "I love to see women working in the kitchen."

"Chauvinist!" She carried the tray into the lounge, sitting down to pour their coffee.

"Not at all." Tim accepted a cup of the steaming liquid. "I've never seen my mother or Claire in a kitchen. I find it very comforting."

Eden sat back, tucking her legs up beneath her. "I don't suppose your mother or sister has ever found it necessary to go into the kitchen; you have more servants than family in your house." Although the Shaws were not exactly in the poverty bracket themselves, Eden had been a little overwhelmed by the unpretentious show of wealth in Tim's parents' home.

Mrs. Channing had welcomed her with all the gracious

politeness that had been bred in her, but Eden had still felt out of her depth in the midst of such opulence. The Channing house was set among the rolling acres that made up the family's estate. Eden had felt her first sense of apprehension as Tim drove the car down the long driveway, unnerved by the prospect of entering the magnificent ranch-style house.

Tim's mother had fitted into the luxury of her background perfectly, coming from an old Southern family. The silk dress was tailored to her slim figure, her gray hair perfectly coiffured, making Eden feel quite underdressed in her trim lemon trousers and matching shirt. Although not by the flicker of an eyelid did Mrs. Channing show that she approved or disapproved of her guest's appearance.

All in all it hadn't been a successful visit, at least as far as Eden was concerned, and it hadn't been something she had ever wanted to repeat, despite Tim's constant pleading. She always had an excuse ready when he suggested they visit his parents.

It had been obvious from the first who was the driving force behind the Channing money; the mild, unassuming Paul Channing certainly could not have made a success of his business without the help of his forceful but charming wife. Tim's mother had no need to enter her kitchen unless she wanted to, the nearest she came to anything domestic being to approve the menus for the day.

Tim came to sit on the sofa beside Eden, his arm around her shoulders as he snuggled her into his side. "I didn't come here to talk about my mother." His mouth caressed her throat. "How would you like to make this a permanent thing?"

Her heart began to beat erratically, and then she cursed herself for jumping to conclusions. He could mean any number of things by that remark—she hoped! "Working in the kitchen?" she teased.

"No, silly," he chuckled. "Will you marry me, Eden?" he asked seriously.

Eden moved back, her worst fears realized. "M-marry you?"

"Will you?" He looked anxious.

"I . . . well, I—I don't know." A nervous laugh caught in her throat. "It's a bit sudden." She stood up to look down at him, wishing he hadn't just asked her to marry him.

"I love you," he said simply. "And I want to marry you. How do you feel about me?"

She wished she knew. Her uncertainty about her feelings was the reason she wished he hadn't proposed. It had never occurred to her that he would ask her to marry him. She enjoyed his company, liked being with him, but marriage . . . ! She wasn't sure she was ready for that.

"I like you," she began slowly. "I like you very much—"

"Enough to marry me?" he cut in eagerly.

"I . . . I'm not sure."

He stood up. "Then how much do you like me?"

"A lot. But marriage—well, that's something different. I have things I want to do before I settle down. I want to travel."

"We could travel together."

Eden shook her head. "Not that sort of travel. I want to just take off for a couple of years, work my way around from place to place. Secretaries are always in demand."

Tim frowned. "You've never talked about this before."

She shrugged. "It wasn't something that came up for discussion."

"And your parents, how do they feel about it?"

She smiled. "They are of the opinion that travel broadens the mind."

"I see." He bit his lip, for once not the confident young man she was used to. "And just when do you propose to 'take off'?"

He was angry; she knew he was angry. "I haven't decided yet," she told him awkwardly.

"But marriage is definitely not part of your plans?"

"Well, not yet. I didn't know you had marriage in mind, Tim," she added almost pleadingly.

His cheeks had an angry flush to them. "What the hell do you think the past six weeks have been about?"

"Well, certainly not marriage."

He gave a harsh laugh. "Believe me, if I didn't have marriage in mind, we would have been finished long ago."

"Meaning?" she challenged, aware that they were having their first argument—and probably their last, by the sound of it. And it had all started from a proposal of marriage!

"Meaning I don't go in for these 'no touching' relationships," he snapped.

"Oh, I see." She was angry now, too. "Well, don't let me keep you. I wouldn't want to stop you from being with someone who feels the way you do about sex." She turned away.

Tim grasped her shoulders, spinning her around to face him. "Hey, come on, Eden. That wasn't what I meant, and you know it. I was just trying to show you that you're special to me."

The tension left her body. "I know. And I'm sorry. But I'm tired, and your proposal was rather a surprise." That was an understatement if ever she had heard one! "I need time to think about it."

"How much time?" he demanded, the harshness back in his voice.

"I don't know. It's not something you can decide on overnight."

"Most people can decide on it straightaway," he snapped, her good-humored companion of the past few weeks not in evidence at all.

"Well, I can't. Or perhaps I can. If my needing time to be sure can make you this bad tempered, I hate to think what you would have done if I'd said a straight no."

He moved to pull on the jacket to his suit. "If I were you I would start your traveling right away. Go to London with Jason to visit your grandfather, see how you like being alone in a country where you know no one. But don't expect me to be waiting for you when you get back!"

"I won't!" Her eyes flashed her anger.

"Good, because I won't be!" He slammed the door on his way out.

She couldn't believe the scene she had just been through. Tim had always seemed so sweet, so mild tempered. He hadn't been mild tempered just now; he had been absolutely furious. He had obviously been upset by her indecision, but she didn't think her reluctance to give him a definite answer should have resulted in that display of outraged anger.

She looked up as the door opened again, forcing a smile to her lips as she saw that her parents had returned home. For a moment she'd thought Tim had come back.

"Have a nice evening?" she asked them.

"Very pleasant," her mother replied, throwing her evening bag onto a chair. "We saw Tim outside. He wasn't his usual composed self."

"Oh," she said lamely. She had hoped she needn't tell her parents of Tim's proposal.

"Have you upset him in some way?" her mother probed.

"I may have done," she evaded the question. Angela wholly approved of Tim and wouldn't be pleased at Eden's refusing to marry him.

"Either you have or you haven't." Her mother's voice was brittle.

"Surely that is their business, Angela," Drew cut in smoothly.

"Don't interfere," his wife ordered. She looked back at Eden. "Have you upset him?"

Drew sighed. "I think I'll go to bed if this is going to turn into one of those long girlish discussions. Don't be too long, darling," he advised his wife.

"Good night, daddy." Eden kissed him warmly on the cheek.

"Angela?" he queried.

"I'll be up in a moment," she told him vaguely. "Now," she pressed her daughter once they were alone, "what happened?"

"I agree with daddy," she said with a frown. "What happens between Tim and me is nobody's affair but our own." She sighed as she saw her mother's agitation rise. "Okay, I'll tell you. I turned down his proposal of marriage, and he didn't like it."

Her mother gasped. "You turned him down?"

"Yes."

"Are you mad?" Angela demanded.

Eden shook her head. "I don't love him."

Her mother gave a harsh laugh. "What does that have to do with it?"

"Quite a lot, I would have thought."

"Then you're a fool. He's heir to so much money you would never have to worry about it again."

"I don't worry about it now," Eden pointed out.

"Only because Drew and I have never let you go without anything. Belive me, I know what it's like." She shuddered in remembrance. "I don't want the hardship for you that I had during my marriage to your father."

"My father wasn't poor."

"He was by the time David Morton had finished with him. David threw him out of the family house, took away his job, everything. We were so poor that—well, we were poor. Your father hated that; he'd always had money. And his father knew it—he knew exactly what to do to get him back into the fold. So you think seriously before you refuse to marry someone like Tim. It isn't easy being poor."

"I've already refused him."

"Then you are a fool. Call him tomorrow and tell him you've changed your mind."

'But I haven't." Nothing her mother had just told her made any difference to how she felt about Tim.

Her mother's eyes narrowed. "Does your refusal have anything to do with Jason Earle and this mad suggestion that you visit your grandfather?"

"Of course not," Eden instantly denied.

"I think it does. But you aren't going to England to visit that old—"

"Mummy—" her voice was mild, effectively hiding her rising anger "—if I want to go to England, then I shall go."

"We'll see about that!" And Angela slammed out of the room.

Eden shook her head dazedly. Now why had she said that? She had no intention of going to England to see David Morton.

CHAPTER THREE

SHE TOLD JASON EARLE AS MUCH when she met him for dinner the next evening. He had called for her as he said he would, leaving the proposed discussion until they had arrived at his hotel and ordered dinner.

He studied her with cool gray eyes, and she was glad she had chosen to wear her one black evening gown, its simplicity of style giving her a sophistication she felt in need of against this man. Her perfectly proportioned body was shown to advantage in the figure-hugging gown, the ribbon shoulder straps displaying a tempting amount of smooth creamy flesh, the curve of her breasts just visible. She wore little makeup, what little she did wear emphasizing her huge golden eyes.

She smiled at the waiter as he placed her chilled melon before her. "I do mean it, Mr. Earle." The smile left her mouth as she looked at him. "England holds no appeal for me whatsoever."

"Not even your grandfather?"

Her wineglass landed with a thud on the table, spilling some of its contents. "Oh, damn," she muttered, beginning to mop up the liquid with her napkin as it rapidly soaked into the snowy white tablecloth.

"Leave it," Jason ordered tersely.

"But it will stain."

He shrugged. "So what?"

"So...I suppose you're right." She threw the napkin

down onto the table, inwardly cursing her awkwardness. "I don't suppose a hotel like this will worry about one stained tablecloth." It was the most exclusive hotel in the area, and she felt sure Jason Earle would be staying in the best suite it had. He had been treated like royalty since their arrival here; and quite frankly, Eden found it a little unnerving. "Not even my grandfather, Mr. Earle," she answered his question. "If David Morton can be called that. He broke my parents' marriage up and then ignored us all these years."

"Your father was his son."

"And does that automatically make me his grand-daughter?"

He sat back. "I would have thought so," he responded, watching her with narrowed eyes.

"I don't agree. Drew is the person who helped bring me up." She gave a bitter smile. "Oh, don't worry, Mr. Earle. When I made that remark about automatically being David Morton's grandchild, I didn't mean there was any doubt about it. My mother was always faithful to my father; it was David Morton who forced them apart."

"That doesn't mean your mother was guiltless."

"No, but it doesn't point to my father's being so, either. I'm sure there were faults on both sides, but I can't forget eighteen years of silence from the grandfather who's never shown that he cared whether I was alive or dead."

"Not even if he's dying?"

Eden paled at the quietly voiced question, swallowing hard. She searched his harsh features for some sign of mockery, some indication that he didn't mean what he said—and found none. His gray eyes were as coldly chilling as usual, his mouth just as cruel. She took a deep breath. "And is he?"

"Yes."

"But I...I don't understand. You didn't mention this to my mother yesterday."

"I think we can assume that David's death is not of great importance to your mother. In fact, she'd likely be glad about it."

"My mother isn't like that!" she snapped. "Why is he dying? I know he's old, but— He can't be dying!"

Jason shrugged. "He recently had a heart attack, and the next one will probably be fatal."

"Oh, God," she groaned.

"Indeed," he agreed. "Not very pleasant."

Her golden eyes were shadowed. "How can you accept it so calmly? I thought he was a friend of yours. Doesn't it affect you at all?"

"Of course it affects me," he said impatiently. "But should you be reacting quite this strongly to news of the impending death of a man who you say means nothing to you?"

She turned her head away. "God, you're cruel," she choked.

Jason stood, pulling her to her feet to maneuver her out of the room with the minimum of effort. Eden looked up as he took her into one of the waiting lifts and pressed the button. "Where are you taking me?" she demanded.

"To my suite," he replied abruptly, keeping a firm hold on her arm.

"Won't that be misconstrued?" she taunted sarcastically, reminding him of his comment of the previous day.

"Possibly. But that would be preferable to your causing a scene in the dining rooom," he added.

She glared up at him, resenting his superior height at that moment. "I wasn't going to cause a scene."

He raised his eyebrows. "Really?"

"Yes, really!" she said crossly. "Obviously what you had just told me came as something of a shock, but—"

"Obviously," he cut in dryly.

"But it was your attitude that upset me!"

He gave her a gentle push out of the lift, moving forward to unlock the door to his suite before ushering her inside. A flick of a switch illuminated the spacious sitting room, the impersonality of its luxury not alleviated by any of this man's personal possessions.

He moved to the extensive array of drinks on the trolley, pouring some amber liquid into a glass before holding it out to her. "Why should my attitude upset you?"

"Because it did." She looked at the glass he had given her. "What's this?"

"Brandy."

She wrinkled her nose. "I don't like brandy."

"I thought it might help you over your apparent shock."

"I'm over it." She put the glassful of liquid down on the table untouched.

"Sit down," he invited.

"No, thank you," she replied stiffly. "Shall we go back downstairs?"

"No."

"No?" She licked her lips nervously.

He shook his head. "I'll ask for the rest of our dinner to be sent up." He picked up the telephone. "We can talk more freely up here."

"That may be so, but I—"

"I don't have any designs on your body," he said impatiently.

Color flooded her cheeks. "I didn't think you had, Mr. Earle."

"Jason, call me Jason. After all, I call you Eden."

"I thought that was a privilege of your age," she taunted.

He showed by a tautening of his mouth that he didn't appreciate her comment, talking into the telephone as he repeated their order for dinner to be sent up to the room. He turned to her. "Let's leave my age out of it. And you might as well sit down; you aren't leaving yet."

"Aren't I?" she challenged.

"No."

She had the feeling he would keep her there by force if she didn't comply, and so she sat down, saving herself the embarrassment of physically losing against him; because she would lose, she knew that. "My gran—David Morton—" She broke off in confusion.

"Your grandfather," he put in softly, standing over her and making her even more nervous.

"David Morton," she said pointedly. "Has he been ill long?"

Jason poured himself a drink before coming to sit in the chair opposite her. "He had the first attack about six weeks ago."

"I see." She bit her lip. It was strange how the man's illness affected her. After all that he had done to her mother, she shouldn't have cared. And yet she did, she did!

"It was a very bad attack," Jason continued. "And the next one could come at any time."

"Probably fatal, you said?"

"That's right." He crossed one leg over the other, stretching them out in front of him. "And he would like to see you before he dies."

This information put her in an intolerable position. She had no wish to go to England, no desire to see her grandfather, but she wasn't normally a vindictive person, didn't like to hurt anyone deliberately, and this appeared to be the wish of a dying man. She had the feeling that Jason Earle knew exactly what pressure he was putting on her, the emotional blackmail that not many people would be able to refuse. His final comment was a deliberate ploy to make her feel guilty; although why she should be made to feel that way, when David Morton had been the one in the wrong all these years, she had no idea. But she did feel guilty—and Jason Earle knew it.

She took a deep breath. "Why should he want to see me?"

"I would have thought that was obvious."

"Not to me. You don't ignore a grandchild all this time and then suddenly decide to take an interest because you have no other family."

"David hasn't ignored you."

Eden stood up to pace the floor in jerky movements. "Then what would you call it?" she turned on him. "And don't tell me he stayed out of my life for my own good, because that just isn't true."

Jason watched her calmly. "Why should you be so sure he has ignored you?"

"Isn't it obvious?"

"Not to me. And not to David, either. When I spoke to him this afternoon—"

"You talked to my—to him this afternoon?" she gasped.

He nodded. "That's right."

"But how? I mean—"

"Have you never heard of the telephone?" he taunted. "They're quite wonderful things. You can just pick one up and talk to—"

"There's no need for sarcasm, Mr. Earle. I'm perfectly well aware of what a telephone is."

"In that case, *Eden*, why be surprised that I've spoken to David? I called him to tell him of your reluctance to visit him. He was upset, naturally, and not a little concerned about your resentment toward him. According to him, your mother may not have been telling you the whole story about the past eighteen years."

She gave him a searching look. "What did he mean?"

"It isn't for me to say. Your mother is the person you should talk to about that."

"Oh, come on. You've gone this far, you might as well finish. In what way has my mother been holding out on me?"

He took his time about answering; finally he shrugged. "You're sure you want to know?"

"Quite sure."

"Okay. Well, it seems that your father kept in touch with your mother during the last years of his life, asked for photographs, things like that. When he died your grandfather kept up these inquiries by telephone."

"Telephone calls about me?"

"Yes."

"I don't believe you."

"Believe the facts. How else could your grandfather know that your best friend at school was Cheryl Sanders, that you came sixth in the History exam you took in fourth grade, that—"

"Okay!" she cried. "But if he knows all that, and my mother obviously told it to him, why has she never mentioned it to me?"

He took a swallow of his drink. "That's something you'll have to ask her."

She picked up her wrap and evening bag, walking hurriedly to the door.

"Where are you going?" Jason was on his feet now.

"To talk to my mother, of course."

"Right now?"

"I can't think of a better time."

He frowned. "But what about dinner? It will be arriving any moment now."

"Then you eat it," she advised tautly. "And don't get

the mistaken idea that anything you've told me makes any difference to me. Even if what you say is true, it doesn't mean I'll go to England."

"Oh, it's true, Eden, and you know it is. But as I've already told you, what you do holds no interest for me. If you decide to make that trip to see David, I'll be glad to make the plane reservation for you."

"I can do that myself—if I think it necessary."

He shrugged. "Please yourself."

"I usually do."

"So I would imagine," he said dryly.

"Meaning what, Mr. Earle?"

"Meaning you come across as a very spoiled little girl."

"Your opinion of me isn't that important to me," she retorted haughtily. "I'm sure I'll survive without your approval."

"I'm sure you will. I'm also sure that when the time comes you'll make Tim an excellent wife."

Her eyes narrowed. "What makes you think I'm going to marry him?"

"You would be a fool if you didn't. Anyone can see he's in love with you."

Eden didn't miss the contempt for the emotion in his voice. "He may be," she accepted. "But it doesn't necessarily follow that I feel the same way about him."

"I wouldn't have thought that was important." He poured himself another drink. "He *was* what you meant when you denied needing your grandfather's money, wasn't he?"

She drew in an angry breath. "No, he was not! Considering you know next to nothing about me, you're very insulting, Mr. Earle."

"You knew even less about me at our first meeting, and yet you already disliked me," he pointed out.

She blushed. "That was different. I knew *of* you."

"And didn't like much of what you'd heard," he mocked.

"Quite," she agreed. "I don't like your taste in women — and I don't mean Claire. Tell me, Mr. Earle, doesn't it bother you that Isobel once stole another woman's husband from her?"

"Why should it bother me? I'm sure we've all got things in our past that we aren't too proud of."

"I'm sure Isobel never regretted marrying my father," she said scornfully.

"As far as I can gather, they were very happy together."

"She's hardly likely to tell you any different; after all, she wouldn't want you to think she wasn't a good wife."

"Being a good wife to someone else doesn't mean that she would be a good one for me. My requirements might be different."

"I can imagine!"

He smiled. "I'm sure you can. But it wasn't from Isobel that I heard the marriage was a success."

"My grandfather, I suppose?"

"Yes."

"The same reasoning applies to him. He angled for that marriage; he was hardly likely to put it down, either."

"Stop being so bitter, girl. That's all in the past. It's the future I'm concerned with."

"Your future with Isobel?"

"If I have any future with her, it's none of your business."

Eden shook her head. "She must know of your reputation, the women you've had, *still* have. But maybe that doesn't bother her. I have no reason to suppose my father was any more faithful to her than he was to my mother. Still, I wouldn't want to be involved with you."

His glance ran insolently over her youthful curves. "You won't get the chance to be. I like my women to be experienced, and you lose out on both counts."

She frowned. "Both?"

"Both. Some girls of twenty have had more lovers than they would care to name. But not you. You're a child, and you definitely aren't experienced."

"How do you know that?"

He smiled, a slow mocking smile, "I know, Eden."

"Then you would be wrong," she told him defiantly. "As you said, a girl doesn't get to twenty nowadays without gaining a little experience."

"How little?" he challenged.

"Not so little," she lied. "Now, if you will excuse me, I really would like to talk to my mother."

"It would appear you have plenty to talk about. And I'll remember your claim to experience; I may have need of it someday."

Eden flushed a fiery red. "Do you ever get that desperate?"

He grinned. "Not with women like Isobel and Claire around."

"You're disgusting!" she snapped. "And boastful."

"Oh, not boastful, Eden. I'm just trying to live up to the reputation you've credited me with."

"I haven't," she denied heatedly. "Everyone else has. The newspapers are always reporting on your activities. After all, you *are* news."

"You flatter me," he taunted.

"Scandalous news, most of the time. Goodbye, Mr. Earle."

"I'll expect to hear from you."

"Don't hold your breath!"

She fumed all the way home in the cab, sure that her

mother would have some reasonable explanation for what he had just told her. She knew her mother felt very bitter toward David Morton, but surely Angela wouldn't have lied to her all this time. And if she had, where did that put Eden in regard to her grandfather?

Drew was alone when she entered the lounge, intent on one of his favorite television programs. "How did your evening go?" he asked interestedly, standing up to turn off the television.

"It didn't." She slumped down into a chair. "We didn't even get as far as having dinner." She hesitated. "Daddy, do you know if my—father and grandfather kept in touch with mummy?"

He looked surprised by the question. "Is that what Jason Earle told you?"

She nodded. "He told me—"

"The truth." Her mother spoke from behind them. She came farther into the room, clothed in a silk bathrobe but with her face still perfectly made up. She was never seen without her full makeup, aware of the few lines that had appeared around her eyes and mouth in recent years.

Eden looked at her sharply. "The truth?"

"Yes, if Mr. Earle told you I heard from Graham until his death, and from David since then."

"You hear from David Morton?" Drew asked slowly.

"Yes," she answered with a certain amount of challenge in her voice.

"How often?" Eden asked.

Her mother shrugged, lighting a cigarette before answering. "Two or three times a year, I suppose."

"Two or three— Mummy!"

"Yes?"

"Angela, is this true?" Drew demanded to know, as shocked as Eden.

"Of course it's true." She gave an abrupt laugh. "Stop looking so surprised, both of you. You didn't think, when Graham's second marriage produced no children, that David would give up his only grandchild, did you, Drew? You should know better than that. He's too selfish to let us get on with the rest of our lives without a reminder from him now and again of his existence."

"But you never mentioned it!" Eden's reproach was obvious.

Her mother's eyes flashed angrily. "Why should I have? A few telephone calls don't make him any less the swine he was when I married your father against his will."

Eden stood up, equally angry. "No, but they prove he hasn't forgotten me."

"I've never said he had. But he didn't make his last call. He always calls on your birthday. This year he missed. I thought—"

"Do you know why he missed it?" Eden cut in shrilly. "He's dying, that's why! He's dying, and all you can think about, all you've ever thought about, is your own bitterness toward him. You had no right to keep his calls from me, no right at all!" She recoiled as Drew's hand snaked out and struck her forcibly across one cheek. "Daddy!" Tears gathered in her eyes.

"Don't ever let me hear you talk to your mother like that again," he told her coldly. "Your grandfather was a swine to your mother when she was married to your father, and whatever she may have done in regard to him since then, she's done for the best, for all of us."

"I'm sorry." Eden cradled her throbbing cheek. "I'm sorry!"

"So you damn well ought to be!"

"Eden." Her mother sounded strange, not at all like the

woman who dominated the household with an iron will. "What's wrong with David?"

"He had a heart attack," she supplied.

"Someone should have let me know—Isobel should have let me know. As he's Eden's grandfather, we had a right to know."

"Perhaps Isobel didn't know about the calls, either," Drew suggested gently.

"She knew," Angela said vehemently. "She tried to stop Graham from making them."

"I think you should lie down," Drew told her sofly, "You're very pale."

"I think I will." She gave a vague smile before going to their bedroom.

Eden watched her go, her frown one of puzzlement. It had never occured to her—nor to Jason, either—that her grandfather's illness would matter to her mother. But it had; Angela looked as if someone had dealt her a blow.

She looked at her stepfather. "Is mummy all right?"

He sighed. "It's just the shock."

"Shock?"

He nodded. "All these years all she's ever had was her hate of David Morton. Oh, she's loved us, in her own way, but it was hate of him that held her together after she had to leave Graham. Knowing he's dying has shocked her to the core."

"But—why?"

"You have to understand your mother to know what she's feeling right now. It's as if her reason for living has been taken away from her. When I married her all those years ago I knew she was still in love with your father, but—"

"Oh, surely not," Eden scorned. "She hated him, as she's always hated his father."

He shook his head sadly. "She's always loved Graham, even after he died. But she couldn't live with him, couldn't live with what David Morton was doing to them both. Your mother is fond of me, and we've had a good marriage, but your father was always the love of her life. She never stopped loving him, even when she knew she had to leave him or make him hate her. And I've never resented the love she had for him; I've accepted it, as I've accepted the affection she has for me."

"I've never realized...."

"No," he smiled. "It wasn't necessary that you should. Don't blame your mother for keeping those calls to herself. The ones she had from Graham I'm sure she kept to herself because they were all she had of him, the only contact she could have with the man she still loved."

"Oh, daddy!" Eden flung herself into his arms. "It must have been awful for you."

"I wouldn't change a minute of it. I've loved your mother and I've loved you, and together we've all been happy."

"But—"

"It's never mattered, Eden, never. Now I'm going to go to her, be her strength. You see, that's the one thing I do know: your mother needs me. And whenever she needs me I intend to be there. Right now she's confused, lost even. If David Morton dies she's going to need me more than ever."

Eden had always known that Drew loved her mother very much, but she had never realized just how selfless that love was. He had known all those years that his wife still loved her first husband, and yet it made no difference to his own love for her.

She should have realized herself how Angela's bitterness and hate for David Morton had always been her strength, her reason for everything she did, the reason she always had to succeed. In her own way she had been proving to David Morton the past eighteen years that she had been good enough for his son; that by rejecting her he had himself lost out. Drew was right: if David Morton died, her mother was going to need him very much.

But what Eden had learned tonight made her want to meet this man, to find out what it was about him that had made her father choose him above his wife and child. And then there was always Isobel Morton. . . .

AND SO IT WAS that Eden found herself on an airplane the next day seated beside Jason Earle, traveling with a man she didn't know, on her way to meet a man she wasn't even sure she wanted to know.

Her mother had raised no further objections, her strangely subdued mother who suddenly seemed to have lost the drive that made her such a strong personality. It was as if all the fight had gone out of her, and for once Eden saw her mother leaning on Drew's quiet strength.

She hadn't wanted to call Jason Earle last night, hadn't wanted to have to listen to the mocking satisfaction she felt sure would be in his voice as he heard of her decision to go to England with him. She had thought of just making her own way there, of not telling him she was going; but that would simply have been a childish gesture, for he would know in the end anyway. Besides, it was going to be a long flight, and although Jason Earle might not be her idea of an ideal companion to pass the hours with, he *was* company. At least, he would have been if he hadn't buried his nose in some papers taken out of his briefcase as soon as they took off.

Eden gave him an impatient look, sighing heavily. She had never doubted for one moment that he would be able to get her a seat on his flight; men like him didn't know the meaning of the word *no*. Besides, who would dare to say it!

Finally she could stand his silence no longer. "You aren't much company, are you," she accused.

Cool gray eyes were turned in her direction as Jason raised his head. "I wasn't aware that you wanted company, especially mine."

Eden flushed at his intended taunt. "I don't suppose it would occur to you that I might be nervous? That I'm traveling to a country I'm not familiar with, to see a man who deprived me of my father?"

"*You* nervous?" he mocked. "I don't believe it."

"That's right," she said scornfully. "Mock me; that's sure to make me feel better." She turned away, her mouth trembling slightly.

Now it was his turn to sigh. "I wasn't mocking your nervousness, I was just surprised that you admitted to such an emotion."

"I'm surprised *you* can be surprised," she snapped.

To her chagrin he gave a throaty chuckle. "You are a constant surprise to me, Eden. You have been since the moment we met."

Against her will her lips began to twitch with humor. "When you thought I would be a child. Just how old did you think I was?" she asked interestedly.

"Eleven or twelve," he admitted ruefully. "Neither David nor Isobel ever mentioned how old you were. I just assumed. But I'm learning that where you're concerned it doesn't pay to *assume* anything. I didn't think you would come with me today. I still don't understand why you have."

She shrugged, still uncertain about that herself. "Curiosity—I think."

"And what about your job? I thought you were a working girl."

"I am. I work for Drew."

"I see."

"Isn't that what stepfathers are for?" she flashed. "To give you time off when you need it? That *is* what you meant, isn't it; that you would hardly call it working when Drew can do without me at such short notice."

"Well, is it?"

"Yes, it is! I don't work for him directly; I work for one of his managers. And I was hired for ability, not through family connections."

"If you say so," he derided her.

"I do! If you ever need a secretary I'll be glad to prove it to you."

His mouth turned back. "I don't envision that happening. Sandra is very capable, and never sick."

"A regular paragon, in fact," Eden taunted.

"Why don't you read a book or something," Jason suggested wearily. "It's too tiring trying to converse with you."

"And you have your work to do!"

"I always deal with my paperwork during the flight; there's usually little else to do."

"Don't let me stop you. I'm sure you have a lot of work to get through, work you should have been doing during the weekend."

"Instead of escorting the lovely Claire," he finished dryly. "Wasn't that the implication?"

"If the shoe fits . . . ."

Jason snapped the lid of his briefcase shut, turning fully to look at her. "Oh, it fits. I believe I've said this before, Eden, but my private life *is* private. I won't attempt to moralize to you if you don't to me."

"Moralize to me?" she gasped. "I have nothing—"

"Not even Tim?" He raised dark eyebrows.

"Certainly not!"

"I thought it was all settled between you two, but Claire tells me her little brother isn't feeling too happy with you at the moment."

"Thought what was settled?" Eden demanded. "Just because I've been dating him for a few weeks doesn't mean I have to jump into bed with him. I'm more discriminating than that."

"I'm glad to hear it. But that wasn't what I meant. First of all Claire informs me you're going to marry her little brother, and then she tells me you've changed your mind."

"I didn't change my mind. I turned him down."

"Why?"

"What business is that of yours?" she asked him moodily.

Jason shrugged. "I'm interested."

"Then channel your interest in another direction. My reasons for not marrying Tim are my own, and I don't intend discussing them with anyone."

"Did the fact that you'll be David's heir when he dies influence your decision in any way?"

Eden was pale with anger, with this man's arrogance, with his—with his.... God, she hated him! "I pity you, Mr. Earle," she told him contemptuously. "How awful to consider every feeling, every relationship, from a monetary angle."

"Not every one, Eden," he taunted coldly. "I was just curious as to why you suddenly changed your mind about marrying Tim."

"I just told you I didn't change my mind; I never intended marrying him. And I don't want my grandfather's money!" Her eyes flashed gold. "I'm with you now only to satisfy the whim of a dying man, and I don't intend staying any longer than I have to."

Jason frowned. "I don't think David envisioned this visit as one of short duration."

"What does he expect? I don't know him and I don't know anyone else in England."

"You know me," he pointed out huskily.

"Hardly," she scoffed lightly. "I met you only a couple of days ago. And I have no idea what Isobel Morton is going to be like."

Those firm, well-shaped lips curved into a smile. "She's the sort of person your grandfather approves of."

"I know that!" She pursed her lips. "Is she beautiful?"

"Very."

"I thought she would be."

"Because she managed to tempt your father away from your mother?"

"No, because you're attracted to her. I can't imagine your thinking of marrying anyone who wasn't beautiful and accomplished. Isobel Morton has to be both those things. After all, you've waited long enough to get married," she added bitchily.

"Thanks! I presume you consider me, at thirty-six, to be in my dotage?"

"Not really." A man like him could never be dismissed as being in his dotage; he was far too dangerously attractive for that! "How old is Isobel?"

"Thirty-eight."

"Doesn't it bother you that she's older than you?"

He shrugged. "Why should it?"

"Of course, you don't love her—you couldn't, and still see Claire—so I don't suppose it matters what age she is."

"And if I said I do love Isobel?"

Eden gave him a scathing glance. "Then I would say you have a lousy idea of love. Doesn't fidelity mean anything to you?"

"There will be plenty of time for that after I'm married."

"So you *are* going to marry her?" she pounced.

"I didn't say Isobel would be my bride," he drawled.

"But she could be?"

"She could be," he nodded. "Look, I thought you wanted to talk," he snapped, "not give me the third degree. Why don't you ask Isobel if she wants to marry *me*? *That* would be interesting to find out."

Eden couldn't see any woman turning him down if finally he decided to marry—especially not a woman of the type she considered Isobel Morton to be.

ISOBEL MORTON was indeed beautiful, Eden had to admit that. Even tearful and distraught she was beautiful, being one of those women who look even more beautiful when ravaged by emotion. Her pale complexion was like porcelain, her petite figure perfectly proportioned, her delicate features perfect, the shoulder-length hair a wavy flame. She looked much younger than her thirty-eight years, her expression tragic as she launched herself into Jason's arms.

She turned to look at Eden from the protection of Jason Earle's embrace, her face now an angry mask, the limpid brown eyes glaring with dislike. "You have to be Eden," she said sneeringly.

"Isobel, what's wrong?" Jason held her at arm's length, searching her features.

"You shouldn't be asking me that," she answered shrilly, her gaze still locked on Eden. "You should be asking that money-grasping little bitch!"

"Isobel!" he cautioned firmly. "What in hell has happened?"

"David is dead!" she screeched. "And all because of *her*!" She looked accusingly at Eden.

CHAPTER FOUR

"D-DEAD?" EDEN ECHOED, her face paling, her legs feeling weak. "But he can't be," she said stupidly.

"But he is," Isobel Morton said harshly. "I know, because I found him."

"Isobel—" Jason took control of the situation "—just explain calmly what happened. We can get into blame and guilt some other time. When did David die?"

"I found him after lunch," she told him, smoothing away her tears. "Let's go into the lounge." She put her hand on his arm. "I'm so glad you're here to take care of everything, Jason."

Eden followed them into the gracious L-shaped lounge as if in a daze. Her grandfather was dead, and she hadn't even had the chance to meet him! Only yesterday she had found out that he did care for her after all, and now he had been taken from her. Fate had dealt her a cruel blow, the cruelest of her life.

She sat down without being asked to, since the conversation she'd had with Isobel Morton so far was hardly welcoming. The woman's shock and distress were understandable, especially as she had found David Morton's body, but that she should blame Eden for the death was not. She had wanted to see her grandfather, get to know him if possible, if only to find out if he truly was the ogre she had always imagined him to be.

"It was too late to let you know, of course," Isobel Morton continued. "Your plane had already taken off."

"I'm sorry I wasn't here." Jason sat beside her on the sofa, his arm still protectively around her shoulders.

"The doctor hasn't been gone long. There was nothing he could do." Her voice broke emotionally. "I couldn't believe it when I found him. He was sitting out in the garden reading and I— Oh, God!" She shuddered against Jason, her face buried in her hands. "It's all *her* fault. It was too much for him, the fact that she was coming here after all this time of not wanting to know."

"Isobel," Jason warned softly. "I know you're upset, but the news has come as a shock to Eden, too. I don't think—"

"Shock!" Isobel echoed scornfully. "Relief, more like. Now she won't have to go through with the charade of acting like the return of the prodigal; now it will all be handed to her with no effort on her part at all. My God, when I think—"

"That's enough!" he ordered sternly.

"Oh, no." She shook her head. "I've hardly started. You know what David's done, that it's all going to be hers? I've stayed here with him all these years, taken care of him even after Graham died, and now everything is to go to her." Her voice had been steadily rising all the way through this tirade until in the end it was at a hysterical pitch. "Well, he's left me this house, and I don't want her in it. Get out," she hissed at Eden. "Just get out!"

Jason caught hold of her as she flew at Eden, immobilizing the hands that had been clenched like talons. He held her struggling body until she became still. "Did the doctor leave you any sedatives, Isobel?" he asked impatiently. "I'm sure he didn't just leave you in this state."

"Yes, he left me some sedatives." Her voice was muffled

against his chest. "But I told him I wouldn't take any until I'd seen you."

"Well, now you've seen me," he said soothingly, beginning to lead her out of the room. "And I think it's time you lay down."

"Yes, darling." Her voice broke again and she leaned on him heavily. "But she isn't staying here. She isn't, Jason!"

"We'll talk about it later."

Eden could hear him talking soothingly to the woman all the way up the stairs. He didn't seem to have any trouble finding the right bedroom, which was perhaps indicative of his role in this household.

Isobel Morton needn't have told her to get out; she had no intention of staying. There was no need for her to stay now, none at all.

She was still sitting numb in the chair when Jason Earle returned to the room fifteen minutes later.

"I'm sorry about that." He sounded preoccupied. "David's death has come as a shock to us all."

"Yes," she acknowledged dully, feeling strangely cold in the heat of the day.

"Isobel isn't normally as rude as that."

"No."

"I'm sure you understand that there are a lot of things to be done. I've asked Mrs. Young to show you to your room," he told her. "I'll be back later."

Eden stood up, her hands clenched at her sides. "Jason?"

"Mmm?" He turned at the door.

"Jason, you aren't leaving me here?" She was unwittingly a forlorn figure in her creased denims and deep pink sweater, her golden eyes suddenly seeming too huge for her pale face.

He looked impatient. "I've just apologized for Isobel's

behavior," he said coldly. "She's in shock. It can't have been pleasant for her finding him like that."

"I realize that—I'm not stupid. But in shock or not, she doesn't want me here—and I can't blame her." She flinched as if in pain. "Was I really responsible for his death?"

"Don't be ridiculous! It's bad enough that Isobel should have said it, but that you should start to believe it...!" He shook his head. "He was looking forward to seeing you, was very excited about it."

"Exactly." She twisted her hands together. "*Was* it too much for him?"

"I would doubt that very much." He looked at his wristwatch. "I really do have to go now. Mrs. Young will take care of you."

"I'm not staying here," Eden told him stubbornly.

"Please don't be difficult, Eden. Your grandfather would have wanted you to stay here."

"But Isobel Morton doesn't want me to, and *I* don't want to," she added desperately. She ran to his side, her hand resting pleadingly on his arm. "Take me with you, Jason. Don't leave me here."

He sighed. "I can't take you with me. Surely you realize—I have the funeral to arrange!"

"Oh. Oh, I see." She bit her bottom lip. "Well, I'm still not staying here. If you insist on leaving me I shall call a taxi and go to a hotel."

"Do you have to be difficult now?" he snapped.

Eden flushed. "I'm not being difficult, I just—"

"Not being difficult!" He was starting to look strained now. "I've already had one hysterical female on my hands; I can do without another."

"I'm not hysterical, Mr. Earle," she said coldly.

"Aren't you?" He quirked one dark eyebrow. "Then you're giving a damned good impression of it."

Tears suddenly filled her golden eyes, a sense of loneliness washing over her. "Please, Jason, you're the only person I know here. The grandfather I never knew just died and I—I'm feeling lost."

"Of course you are." He pulled her into his arms, her head resting on his shoulder. "I'm sorry. Put my churlishness down to my own sense of loss. David was a friend of mine for some time, and his death has taken me by surprise."

"I—"

"Well, well, now, isn't this cozy?" Isobel Morton was watching them from halfway up the stairs. "Not content with killing your own grandfather, you're now trying to take Jason away from me."

"Oh, God!" Jason groaned softly, turning to push Eden back into the lounge. "Wait for me there," he ordered. "I won't be long."

"But—"

"Wait for me, Eden!" He shut the door in her face.

He was back within minutes, looking no less the assured man she had become accustomed to the past two days, a man completely in control of any situation, including this one.

"Okay," he sighed. "Get your case and we'll go."

"Oh, thank you!" She gave him a tremulous smile. "I'm very grateful."

"The state Isobel is in at the moment, she can only get more insulting. It wouldn't be wise to leave you here." He gave her a searching look. "What's wrong now?"

She nibbled the inside of her mouth. "I'll have to let my mother know."

"So?" He frowned.

"So...never mind, you wouldn't understand."

"Try me."

"She— No, you really wouldn't understand. Sufficient to say, telling her isn't going to be easy," she said, grimacing.

"Death is never pleasant."

"No," she quietly agreed, bowing her head. "I—I think I'll call Drew and let him break the news to her."

"I can't believe your mother would care one way or the other," he said dismissively. "After all, once she married your stepfather she took on a new father-in-law."

"As I said, you wouldn't understand."

She stared rigidly ahead as he drove through the London traffic. "Where are you taking me?"

He shrugged. "To my home, where else?"

"*Your* home?" She looked at him with startled eyes.

He nodded. "I have a house not far from here."

"But I thought—"

"Yes?" he prompted.

She looked slightly guilty. "I thought you lived there—with her."

He gave a grim smile. "Well, now you know I don't," he said tersely.

"Sorry," she mumbled. "I didn't mean—I'm sorry."

"Forget it. We're all a bit strained. I'm sorry you didn't get to meet your grandfather. I think you would have liked him, for all of his domineering ways."

"Maybe," she agreed gruffly. "Jason, what do I do now?" It was amazing how easily she had slipped onto this first-name basis with him, but in the crisis in which they found themselves, formality seemed ridiculous.

"Right now or long term?"

"Both, I suppose."

"Right now you stay with me. I have a housekeeper who will be an adequate chaperone." He laughed as he saw her expression. "The fact that your grandfather just died wouldn't mean a thing to most people."

"Then perhaps I should go to a hotel as I intended to do."

"No," he said sharply, "you stay with me. It's more convenient that way. The long term... well, you'll just have to wait and see. Isobel was right—David has left you everything but the house and a nominal yearly sum for her. You'll have to stay in England to sort all that out."

Eden frowned. "But I know nothing about high finance," she protested. "Left to me, everything he worked for would be lost within a few weeks."

"He left provision for that."

"He did?"

"Mmm." Jason swung the car in down a long gravel driveway, the huge house that he called home on a main road but far enough back and sufficiently shielded by the trees to offer great privacy. "We'll talk about that some other time," he said as he helped her out of the car. "Mrs. Gifford will take care of you now. I have some calls to make."

Mrs. Gifford turned out to be a plump homely woman who instantly took Eden under her wing when informed by Jason of the situation. Eden felt grateful for the older woman's gentle firmness as she showed her into a bedroom, leaving her only long enough to warm her some soup. After that she insisted Eden go to bed, tucking her in and staying with her until she fell asleep, almost as if she were her mother—except that her real mother had never done such maternal things.

The soup had thawed her numb feelings somwhat, and she realized what a coward she was being. She had more or less begged Jason Earle to bring her here! She should have insisted he take her to a hotel as she had originally intended. She certainly couldn't stay here as a guest, not as the guest of a man she hated....

IT WAS DARK when she woke up, but a side lamp had been left on so that the room wasn't in complete darkness. The house seemed very quiet, almost as if she were completely alone. But she couldn't be—could she?

She sat up in panic, swinging her legs to the floor before running down the stairs and into the lounge. It was in darkness, the whole house was in darkness! A sob caught in her throat and she sank down onto the carpeted floor. How could Jason be this cruel, how could he?

"What the hell...!" Strong arms reached down and pulled her to her feet, familiar arms that had held her once before today. "What were you doing down there?" Jason demanded to know.

Her eyes showed her relief as she gazed desperately into his concerned face.

"Oh, Jason," she sobbed, holding on to him tightly. "I thought you had left me here. I thought I was alone."

"You stupid child," he said harshly. "I've been in my study for the past two hours. Mrs. Gifford has retired for the night."

Her head rested on his shoulder, her short golden cap of hair splayed out on the dark brown shirt he wore. She drew a ragged breath. "I just thought—"

"You thought I was swine enough to leave you completely alone at a time like this," he finished grimly.

"No! I—I just thought you had gone to Isobel, who needs you more."

"I'm not so sure she does. She's sleeping through the worst of her shock, while you're very much awake."

She suddenly became aware of where she was, of the way her hands were clinging to the back of his neck. She tried to pull away. "I'm sorry," she mumbled. "I—"

"Stay where you are," he ordered gruffly.

"But—"

"Don't move, Eden!" His command wouldn't be denied. "You aren't that innocent that you don't know when it's wisest to say and do nothing."

No, she wasn't that innocent. Something was happening between them, something tangibly physical, Jason's sudden awareness of her as easily discernable as her own heightened emotions. That was the trouble, of course—emotions were running high at the moment, an ideal situation for things to get out of control. Her own control had wavered slightly the moment Jason took her in his arms.

Finally he put her away from him, his mouth a grim angry line. "Come with me," he instructed.

She hung back, her trepidation unhidden in her clear golden eyes. "I don't—"

"Don't think you should?" his voice taunted, those steely eyes cruelly appraising. "I'm not going to take you to my bed or anything remotely like that," he mocked. "I'm not going to pretend that the idea didn't cross my mind just now, but I believe we agreed that would happen only through an act of desperation on my part. I don't happen to be that desperate just yet."

Eden had paled more and more as each cruel word left that well-shaped mouth, until now she was a sickly gray color. She was all the more bewildered and hurt because in the past few minutes she had become aware of Jason Earle in a way she had been aware of no other man, not even Tim. Every muscle and sinew of this man, every harsh feature, suddenly attracted her as nothing else ever had.

But she didn't like him, didn't like his arrogance, the easy way he accepted the adoration of women like Claire and Isobel. Then why this sudden attraction? She had heard of a purely physical response to someone, but she had never believed she would fall a victim to it.

She gave Jason a sharp look. Did he know of her sudden change of emotion toward him? Oh, God, she hoped not. Anyway, it wouldn't last. Physical infatuation never did—or so she had been told!

"Eden!"

The sharpness of his tone brought her momentarily to her senses. "Sorry?"

He gave an impatient sigh. "Come to my study."

She trailed after him when it appeared that was what she expected her to do. He poured some brandy and handed it to her. "This seems to be becoming a habit," she said ruefully, bowing her head, her confusion still evident in her shadowed eyes, a confusion she didn't want Jason to see.

"What does?" he queried absently, seated behind the huge mahogany desk now, suddenly the remote figure of their first meeting.

"You plying me with brandy." She attempted a light laugh, aware by the narrowing of his gray eyes that she hadn't succeeded in convincing him of her composure.

"I'm not 'plying' you with anything," he stated distantly. "On the two occasions I've offered you brandy you seem to have been suffering from shock."

"Good heavens, how you do dramatize. Being in a man's arms isn't exactly a new experience for me," she told him. "Hardly likely to cause shock—even if they were the arms of the famous Jason Earle."

"That wasn't the shock I meant," he said coldly, icy disdain in every feature of that harsh face. "I was referring to the shock of your grandfather's death."

"Oh." She blushed scarlet. "Oh, yes. I—I'd forgotten for the moment," she admitted almost guiltily.

Jason shrugged. "That isn't surprising. You didn't even know David."

"But I should feel something!"

"Don't torture yourself with guilt over feelings that simply can't exist."

"But he *was* my grandfather." Tears shimmered in her golden eyes for her lack of emotion.

"He was that, all right," Jason mused. "I don't know why I didn't realize it the first time I saw you, maybe because I was looking at the body and not the eyes. His eyes were that color, too."

Eden blushed at his admission of looking at her body. "Th-they were?" It seemed strange to have inherited the coloring of a man who had only been a stranger to her, a man her mother had brought her up to hate and despise.

He nodded, his penetrating gaze still fixed on her pale face. "In David they were more of a tawny color, not gold, but they're definitely his eyes."

Eyes that all life had faded from. Eden could feel the sadness for the passing of life even if she couldn't feel the sadness for the loss of a grandfather. "What was he like?" she queried softly.

"Do you thing that's a fair question to ask me? I can see him only from a man's point of view, as a friend and business colleague."

"Whatever point of view you see him from, it will still be a hundred percent better than the one I have," she snapped.

"Okay," he sighed. "Point taken. Hasn't your mother talked about him to you?"

Only to criticize him! But how could Eden explain to this cynical man that her mother had been so wrapped up in her bitterness that it colored every statement she ever made about David Morton; that the bitterness had grown and festered until only the possibility of his death had shown her the futility of her emotions. This man couldn't even begin to understand.

"My mother hadn't seen him for eighteen years; he must have changed drastically in that time," she answered evasively.

"I would presume so," he mocked.

"Well?"

He shrugged, leaning back thoughtfully. "He was a man who knew what he wanted at all times, went all out to get it. Until his illness he was still an astute businessman, completely ruthless, very successful at what he did."

"That sounds like a description of you," she said dryly.

"Maybe," he acknowledged harshly.

"Although you've been kind to me, too," she added contritely.

"Kinder than you ever thought I could be," he mocked. "But I exacted payment, didn't I?"

Her eyes widened apprehensively. After all, she was completely at his mercy alone here with him in his house. Had she been too trusting? The predatory look in his eyes seemed to indicate as much.

Suddenly he laughed, a cruel taunting laugh that was meant to wound—and did. "Don't worry, Eden. I'm just teasing you. You're way out of your league with me; you would be better to stick to meek little lapdogs like Tim Channing."

"Tim isn't a lapdog!" Some of her defiant anger came to the fore to save her from utter humiliation. This man had known of her temporary weakness toward him, knew of it and was warning her that she wouldn't get off so lightly if the experience were ever repeated. "He's worth ten of you," she added for good measure.

"Then why aren't you marrying him?"

"I just may do that!" She stood up to glare at him, feeling at a disadvantage seated across the formality of the desk. "When I get back to the States I just might marry him."

"Ah, yes." He pursed his lips. "When you get back."

Eden frowned, not liking the way he had said that at all. "What do you mean, *when* I get back?" she asked suspiciously.

"You said it first," he reminded her calmly.

"Not the way you did. You seemed to imply that it would be some time before I went home."

"Did I? Purely unintentionally, I can assure you."

"Can you?" she persisted. "It sounded that way to me."

"I think we can agree that you aren't a very good judge of anything at the moment," Jason said insultingly. "But perhaps it would be better to ask Tim to visit you over here, if you have to see him. We'll have things to sort out over here in the next few weeks."

"What sort of things?"

"Your inheritance, for one thing."

She grimaced. "Not now, Jason. It's in rather bad taste."

"You brought it up. But you may as well know now that you won't be able to go anywhere until it's all been settled."

"I don't want anything. My grandfather owed me nothing."

"I don't think he considered he *owed* you anything, either," Jason said dryly. "But nevertheless it's yours. You can't just walk away from that."

"I can. I—"

"Don't be such a selfish little bitch," he snapped. "You ignored your father and grandfather for—"

"*I* ignored them?" she cut in indignantly. "I did no such thing! They—"

"Oh, yes, you did. It worked both ways, Eden. Okay, so they rejected your mother, but that rejection didn't include you. You had ample opportunity to visit David, and he can only have been hurt by your tardiness. I think the least you can do is give David a little of your time now that he's dead."

"You don't pull your punches, do you," she choked.

"Did you expect me to?"

"No."

"Then I'm glad you weren't disappointed."

"Have you—have you seen Isobel?"

His mouth tightened into a grim line. "Yes, I've seen her."

"She hasn't calmed down," Eden said knowingly.

"Oh, she's calm enough—too calm. When she breaks I just hope you aren't in the firing line."

"Another reason for me to leave. She can't want me here, her husband's child by his first marriage."

"She doesn't have a say in it. And you aren't going anywhere." He stood up, his powerful body dominating—and attracting. Oh, God, this couldn't be happening to her. "Not until I say you can."

"Until *you*...?" Eden saw red angry spots of color entering her cheeks. "Just who the hell do you think you are? Until *you* say!" she repeated disbelievingly. "You might have women like Isobel Morton and Claire Channing hanging onto your every word, but I don't respond to arrogance."

"No." His humorless smile taunted her. "I think we've established what you respond to."

"Why you—"

"I wouldn't do that," he warned calmly as she went to hit him. "*I* don't respond well to violence. I would retaliate in a way that I would find infinitely satisfying, but you might find less pleasant."

Eden swallowed hard, her raised hand slowly falling back to her side. "You mean...."

"No, I do not mean!" he bit out coldly. "I would put you

over my knee and give you the spanking you deserve. *Then* I just might kiss you." He smiled mockingly.

"Oh, I see." The scorn in her tone was intended to hide her fear. If he should kiss her...! "That's the sort of thing that turns you on, is it?"

She knew she had gone too far by the angry glitter in his gray eyes and the sudden tightening of his mouth. "No," he said grimly. "That isn't what turns me on." He pulled her roughly into his arms. "*This* is what turns me on," he murmured before his mouth descended on hers.

All of her struggles were to no avail as he punished her mouth with slow ruthlessness, grinding her lips against her teeth as she stubbornly refused to open her mouth. She had invited this onslaught, but that didn't make it any easier to bear.

And then the pressure of his mouth on hers changed, became more insistently persuasive, and it was done so subtly that Eden didn't even realize she had begun to respond. That he was an expert lover she was in no doubt, seeming to draw the very soul from her with the deep intimacy of his kiss, his hands slowly caressing her body from breast to thigh, holding her hips firmly against his thighs and making her wholly aware of his renewed arousal.

At last he released her, stepping back to survey her flushed cheeks and fever-bright eyes with undisguised satisfaction. "Yes," he murmured softly. "That's what turns me on."

She didn't need to be told that; his desire had been in every tensed muscle of his body, his mouth telling her what he really wanted to do. And that certainly hadn't been just to kiss her!

She put up a hand to her tousled hair, aware that it had been Jason's hands in her hair, holding her immovable for his kiss, that had caused the disorder. "You're disgusting!"

she snapped defensively. "How dare you kiss me like that when you're going to marry another woman?"

He raised dark eyebrows. "*I* am?"

"You know you are. Isobel Morton!"

"I wasn't aware that you owed any loyalty to Isobel."

"After what she did to my mother, I don't. But—"

"Then leave the feelings of guilt to me—if I feel them necessary."

"Which you don't!"

"As I have no intention of marrying Isobel, no."

"But you—"

"Shouldn't you call your mother?" he cut in tersely. "You said she would want to know."

"Oh, God, yes. I'd forgotten." In the force of his love-making she had forgotten everything!

The narrowing of his eyes seemed to tell her he knew that. "Would you like me to make the call for you?"

"No," she sighed. "This is something I have to do for myself."

Jason shrugged. "If you insist...."

"I do," she said firmly. "Can I make the call from here?"

"Or the lounge, or your bedroom. Take your pick," he told her.

"I didn't mean that. I meant, can I make the call from your house?"

His gaze swept over her with slow deliberation, mockery in every harsh feature. "Worried about what I might ask in payment for using the telephone?" he taunted, a smile on his lips.

"No!" Why did this man have the power to reduce her to the level of a gauche schoolgirl? He wasn't the first sophisticated, self-assured, utterly arrogant man she had ever met, and yet.... She shouldn't be attracted to him, should feel only dislike for him. But all she did feel was a longing to be back in his arms.

But she wouldn't think of that now, couldn't think of it now. If she was to continue to live in this house for the next few days at least, then the sudden awareness that had sprung up between them would have to be dampened down. Not that he seemed to care whether it was or not! He wasn't above enjoying a little flirtation with her. But she had the feeling that on her side there would be nothing light about it.

She gave him a challenging look. "Can I make the call from here or not?" she demanded.

"Be my guest," he drawled. "Or whatever else you want to be," he added huskily. "I'm open to offers."

"If I have to pay for my room and board in that way, I would rather go to a hotel!" she lied.

He was still smiling that infuriating smile. "You don't *have* to do anything. I was just wondering whether you would care to share your room."

"No, I wouldn't," she told him stiffly.

"Not used to waking up and finding the man still in bed with you in the morning?" he taunted.

"That's right!" Eden snapped angrily. "I prefer to sleep alone."

"Now that's a pity, because I like waking up and finding someone in bed with me."

"I'm sure that happens all too often."

"Too true," he smiled. "That way you can repeat the experience of the night before."

"Really?" She adopted a blasé attitude, sure that this man had slept with more women than he cared to remember—and she didn't like it one bit. "I've always found it's never a repeat; each time is a new experience."

He raised his eyebrows. "In that case perhaps you should

accept Tim's offer of marriage. You sound as if you have the ideal physical relationship.''

"I don't think I mentioned Tim's name. I find each time a new experience because I always make sure it's a different man,'' she added in a bored voice.

"I can't believe that,'' he scoffed. "You don't appear to be that type of—''

"What type, Mr. Earle?'' she asked, her voice dangerously soft, his attitude egging her on to further outrageous lies. "Is it only the man's prerogative to experiment? I want to experience as much as I can in my life before I finally settle down with one man.''

"But you don't want one of those experiences to be with me?''

"No!''

"Not even as a means of paying Isobel back for marrying your father?''

"Do what she did to my mother, you mean—take her man away from her?''

He nodded. "That's the idea.''

"There are plenty of available men without poaching on another woman's property. I wouldn't reduce myself to her level.''

"I already told you I belong to no woman!'' His voice had hardened into anger.

"Perhaps that's your trouble, Mr. Earle. You can't accept that at your age you should be turning your thoughts toward a settled home and family, not trying to get every female you meet into bed with you.'' She looked at him with wide innocent eyes, pretending not to notice how her barbs angered him. "After all, you are old enough to be my father.''

"And you're young enough to have that spanking I mentioned earlier.'' He took a threatening step toward her.

"Oh, no, Mr. Earle." She put her hand on his chest, giving a deliberately provocative laugh. "I remember what you said would follow the spanking, and I'd rather not repeat that. *You* don't turn *me* on."

"Why you little—"

"Can't you take rejection gracefully?" she asked regretfully. "I do so hate it when a man makes a scene about these things."

"One of these days ..." he warned viciously. "One day you might be called upon to prove your claim to experience."

"Only if you get desperate," she reminded him sweetly. "You seem to be an experienced lover," she added musingly. "But then, that doesn't mean you're any good at it," she finished tauntingly.

His eyes had narrowed angrily. "I'm warning you, Eden!"

"Yes," she nodded. "One of these days. Well, we'll have to see about that. You never know, *I* might get that desperate. After all, I don't know any men in London."

"I'm sure you'll soon rectify that situation," he said grimly.

"No doubt." She gave him a bright smile. "I'll call my mother from my bedroom, I think. I'll see you in the morning, shall I?" She could see this conversation hadn't pleased him at all. Well, it served him right for being so damned sure of himself—and her response to him.

"Perhaps." He nodded distantly. "Although I may have already left for the office by the time you come down."

Her eyes widened at that. "You're going to *work* in the morning?"

"I have to. There's no need to look like that, Eden. Your grandfather may be dead, but the rest of life has to go on. I'm sorry you'll be here alone, but—"

"I wasn't thinking of myself," she told him coldly.

"Isobel?"

"Yes."

"I will, of course, be spending part of tomorrow with her, but she'll still be under sedation most of the day. My time can be better employed at the office."

"I'm sure it can," she said bitterly.

"You don't understand, Eden. But you soon will."

"That sounds like a threat." Her look was defiant.

"Go and make your call," he said impatiently. "But don't give your mother any false hopes about your return. It just isn't possible at the moment."

"I shall go home when I damn well feel like it!"

Jason's eyes narrowed. "We'll see, shall we?"

CHAPTER FIVE

UNFORTUNATELY, DREW WASN'T AT HOME when she tele-phoned, but the maid recognized her voice and so she had to ask to speak to her mother or make matters worse.

"You've certainly taken your time about calling me," came her mother's waspish comment. "I've been waiting hours for your call."

"Sorry, mummy." Her tongue felt as if it were stuck to the roof of her mouth. She couldn't not tell her mother what had happened, but she just wished Drew could have been there.

"Well?" There was a noticeable tension in her mother's voice. "Don't keep me in suspense, Eden. Have you seen David yet?"

"I—"

"Of course you'll have seen him," her mother answered her own question. "How is he?"

"Mummy—"

"He must be very ill, I realize that," she muttered. "But I just can't imagine him going to die."

"Mummy—"

"Just a minute, Eden. Drew just came in."

"He did?" She almost sighed with relief. "Can I talk to him?"

"Not right now. Hello, darling." She was obviously talk-ing to her husband. "Now, Eden, tell me how you're get-ting on with David," she demanded to know.

"Mummy, could I please talk to Drew?"

"Eden?" her mother queried sharply. "Eden, what's happened?"

"Just let me talk to Drew," she pleaded.

"No!" Her mother's denial came over shrill. "Tell me what's wrong."

"I—"

"Need any help?" Jason stood in the open doorway of her bedroom.

"Oh, God, yes!" Eden groaned. "Just a minute, mummy," she said hastily. "Jason wants a word with me."

"Jason?" her mother echoed sharply. "What's Jason Earle doing there?"

"Just a minute, mummy," she repeated, putting her hand over the mouthpiece. "I can't tell her," she groaned pleadingly.

"That's what I thought." He came into the room. "I overheard your desperation on my way to my room. Let me do it." He put out a hand for the receiver.

"No! No, you—you don't realize what it will do to her."

"I'm beginning to. Give me the phone, Eden," he ordered.

"Eden? Eden!" Her mother's distressed voice came over the telephone. "Eden, are you still there?"

She was torn in two, not wanting to tell her mother herself and yet not wanting Jason to callously break the news to her, either. As Drew had pointed out, David Morton had been her mother's driving force. Finally she thrust the receiver at Jason. "Ask to speak to Drew," she hissed. "He'll know what to do."

"Mrs. Shaw?" He took over calmly. "Would you put your husband on? *Now*, Mrs. Shaw," he added firmly.

Her mother must have recognized Jason's superior authority, because seconds later he was talking to Drew. He explained the situation calmly and precisely, with none of the emotionalism Eden had displayed.

"No, Eden won't be returning yet," she heard him tell Drew. "Not for several months, I'm afraid."

Several *months*! What was he talking about? "Jason—"

He raised his hand to silence her, his dark frown a warning. "And in the circumstances," he continued, "I think you may as well employ someone else to take her place."

"How dare—"

"Yes, of course I understand you have to go now." Jason deliberately turned his back on her. "No doubt Eden will be in touch again later on." He put the telephone down.

Eden's eyes sparkled with golden brightness. "What do you mean by telling Drew to give someone else my job?" she demanded. "I need that job, I *like* that job. And what's this about my staying here several months? I'm not staying here that long."

"Stop arguing with me, Eden." He ran a tired hand over his eyes. "One way and another it's been quite a day."

"I'm sure it has. But you can't just take over my life like that. You should have let me talk to Drew."

"You can talk to him some other time, and your mother sounded as if she was becoming hysterical."

"Oh." That didn't surprise her in the least. "But you should still have—"

"For God's sake, Eden! Just leave it for now, will you? Talk to me about it tomorrow, when I'm feeling more able to explain things to you."

"I'd rather know now," she told him crossly.

"No doubt," he accepted wearily, lines of strain visible beside his nose and mouth. "But I'm too damned tired to think about anything but going to bed right now." He gave a grim smile. "If you let me share your bed tonight I can assure you all I would want to do would be sleep."

Color flooded her cheeks, but she supposed she had asked for that sort of remark by her behavior in his study. "I would be more worried about when you woke up in the morning."

"Mmm," he nodded. "There is that. Oh, well, it was just an idea. If you should change your mind I'm two doors up. Don't hesitate to knock," he taunted.

"I'm not in the habit of visiting men's bedrooms," she told him haughtily.

He shrugged. "It's an open invitation. I'll see you sometime tomorrow, then."

"Yes," she acknowledged huskily.

She had brought this situation on herself. If only Jason hadn't angered her so much that she had told him all those lies about herself, pretending a way of life she abhorred. She had nothing against unmarried couples sleeping together if they were in love with each other, but she despised the people who hopped in and out of bed with anyone they considered attractive. A lot of the men she had been out with in the past had considered going to bed together a natural occurrence after the second or third date, an illusion she had quickly broken. And now she was attracted to someone who didn't even pretend he wanted to date her first!

Her own attitude had changed dramatically toward Jason in the past twenty-four hours; her thoughts of him were all confused. But if she had changed, so had he, making no secret of his instant desire for her.

As Jason had predicted, he had already left for work when she came downstairs the next day for breakfast. Mrs. Gifford saw to her needs with quiet efficiency, leaving Eden alone in the lounge when she had finished her meal.

Eden picked up the paperback that lay on the coffee

table, flicking through the pages before putting it down again with a grimace. Political intrigues weren't to her taste, although she could understand their appeal for Jason; he had the sort of quick agile mind that could appreciate such things.

She had come down early with the expectation of finding him still at home, and it was only nine o'clock now. What was she supposed to do all day?

She looked up as Mrs. Gifford came in with the daily newspaper. Oh, well, it would be something to read. She took the publication gratefully. "Does Mr. Earle come home for lunch?" she asked casually. Any company would be better than being alone like this!

"Sometimes," the housekeeper smiled. "But he mainly lunches at his club, unless he has a luncheon appointment, of course."

"Do you have any idea what he's doing today?"

"I'm afraid not, Miss Shaw. Usually he tells me at breakfast what his plans are for meals, but with the upset of Mr. Morton—of your grandfather—he must have forgotten."

"Yes," Eden nodded. "Thank you anyway."

"Will you be in to lunch, Miss Shaw?"

Would she be in to lunch? Her first instinct was to say yes; she didn't think Jason would appreciate her going out and wandering around on her own. But then she changed her mind. She couldn't mope around there all day alone. "No, I don't think so, Mrs. Gifford. I, er, I think I'll go for a walk."

"What shall I tell Mr. Earle if he does come home for lunch?"

Eden hesitated, knowing that Jason wouldn't like her to be going out. "Tell him I should be back in time for dinner." Her tone was deliberately careless.

Mrs. Gifford frowned. "I'm not sure you should be going

out on your own. London isn't what you're used to, and I wouldn't want you to get lost."

The poor woman probably thought they still lived in shacks in one-horse towns in the States! "Don't worry—" she gave her most endearing smile "—if I do get lost I'll make sure Mr. Earle knows you warned me against it."

"That wasn't what I meant."

She realized the housekeeper suspected her of doing something stupid because of the sudden death of her grandfather. The poor women couldn't know that she had never met him. "I'll take care, Mrs. Gifford," she said gently. "I'll write the telephone number down so that I can call you if I need help."

"Very well." But it was obvious she still didn't approve.

"Did you—did you know my grandfather, Mrs. Gifford?" Eden asked shyly.

"Oh, yes," the housekeeper smiled. "He and Mrs. Morton often came here to dinner."

"Oh, yes, yes, of course." For a while she had forgotten Isobel Morton's existence. That was probably due to the fact that last night Jason seemed to have done the same thing.

He had said he had no intention of marrying Isobel Morton, and yet the housekeeper seemed to give the impression that he they were very close indeed. Mrs. Gifford had made her wonder how frequent a visitor Isobel Morton was to Jason's house. Maybe they slept together here, in the bedroom Jason had invited Eden to last night!

She still blushed when she remembered how things had changed between herself and Jason last night, her feelings toward him especially. She had caught a brief glimpse of some of that other eighty percent of the iceberg Drew had once described him as—and the sensual warmth he had shown her had taken her breath away.

She could now better understand Claire Channing's completely out-of-character behavior toward him, for her own behavior hadn't been normal, either. The lies she had told as a form of defense were proof of that. She *would* go for that walk, would look at the shops and take her mind off the confusion Jason had thrown her into.

She collected a black leather jacket from her bedroom and put it on over her pale lemon long-sleeved sweater and matching lemon denims, both of these articles of clothing fitting her like a second skin. She had no doubt Jason would raise a disapproving eyebrow when he saw how she dressed — and maybe that was why she had put these clothes on.

Oh, damn Jason Earle and his disapproval! Why should his opinion matter to her, anyway? He was nothing to her, nothing but an arrogant man who had to captivate every female he came across. She wished she could be the exception, but she had the feeling that, far from being immune to him, she was going to find him only too attractive.

"Are you off now?" Mrs. Gifford was watching her exit.

Eden gave her a friendly smile. "Yes. Would you like me to get you anything while I'm out?"

The housekeeper looked taken aback. "No, thank you, Miss Shaw. We have our groceries delivered."

"Oh, I didn't mean groceries," Eden chuckled. "I meant, did *you* want anything?"

"Me?" Mrs. Gifford looked even more astounded. "Why, no, I don't think—"

"Sorry," Eden laughed. "I forget things like that aren't done over here. Back home I often do some shopping for our housekeeper."

"Well, I'm sure it's nice of you to offer... but no, I don't think so. Thank you," she added shyly.

"Okay," Eden shrugged. "See you." And she let herself out.

She soon found that Mrs. Gifford was right: London wasn't what she was used to. The shops were interesting, but the people...! They all seemed to be on their way somewhere and were apparently late for their appointments. Whatever their reason, she was jostled and knocked about so much that her pleasure in the shops was ruined. She finally bought herself a sandwich and a can of Coke and escaped to the relative peace of one of the parks. She would have to get a taxi back to Jason's home from here, for she had no idea of the way.

She ate half of the ham sandwich, sitting on a bench to feed the rest to the hungry pigeons. They were a greedy lot, and the rest of her sandwich quickly disappeared down their avid beaks. "All gone," she laughed as they still fluttered around her feet, looking at her with the most appealing eyes. She tipped the bag up as if to show them it was empty.

"They won't go away," remarked a voice from the bench opposite her. "Not until someone else starts feeding them."

Eden looked interestedly at the young man seated across the pathway from her. When he had sat down a few minutes earlier she had subconsciously noted that he was young, quite attractive. A closer inspection revealed that he was more than just quite attractive, he was very good-looking. He was dressed as casually as she was, in denims and a T-shirt, his blond hair worn long but not in the least untidy. He was probably a year or two older that she was.

He grinned at her, his teeth firm and white, his blue eyes sparkling. "Come and sit over here," he invited. "They won't follow you."

"Sure?" she laughed.

"Mmm," he nodded. "They're too busy pecking around for any little crumb they may have missed the first time. Come over here and see."

The pigeons scattered as she walked through them, but the young man was right: they didn't attempt to follow her. She sat down beside him. "I was beginning to feel hounded," she laughed.

"They have that effect on you. I often used to come here to eat, but now I don't bother. It's a good way of dieting. I'm Gary Nichols," he added with a smile.

"Nice to meet you, Gary." She smiled back. "I'm Eden Shaw."

"Have you been over here long?"

She grinned. "That obvious, hmm?"

"Well...."

"In the States I get teased about my English-sounding accent," she said with a wry shake of her head. "Over here I'm easily recognizable as being an American. I can't win."

"You originally come from England?"

She nodded. "A very long time ago." She was beginning to feel a little ashamed of herself, talking to a complete stranger. She stood up. "I think I should be going now."

Gary fell into step beside her. "Do you have to go?" His hand rested lightly on her arm. "I have the afternoon free and I—well, I'd like to spend it with you."

Eden's eyes widened to golden orbs. "I don't think so, thank you." He seemed pleasant enough, but that didn't mean he was. He could be a rapist for all she knew!

"We'll stay within eyeshot and earshot of people," he said as if guessing her thoughts.

Eden laughed. "Sorry. I didn't mean to be that obvious."

"That isn't being obvious, that's just being sensible. Let's go and have a coffee somewhere, shall we? We can sit and talk then."

She hesitated. It would be a way of passing some of this surplus time, and he did seem very nice.... "Okay," she agreed. "Just for a few minutes," she added warningly.

"Good. Come on—I know of a great place not far from here."

Shortly after, in a comfortable nearby café, Eden sat stirring her coffee; not because she had added sugar—she didn't take it—but because she was a little uncertain of her willingness to be with this young man, charming as he appeared on the surface. For a girl who usually liked to get to know someone before even agreeing to go out with him, her behavior was rather strange. But then, everything that had happened since her arrival in England had been strange, and talking to Gary Nichols was just a continuance of events.

"I sat on that bench deliberately, you know."

Eden looked up with a start, finding curious blue eyes watching her intently. "Sorry?"

"That bench in the park—I sat there on purpose. I was only on my way through, really, taking a shortcut from a friend's flat, and then I saw you. I wanted to get to know you."

His frankness didn't surprise her, for he seemed a very forthright young man. Looking at him she realized why she had allowed him to talk to her, why she had latched onto him as if he were the only other human being in a desert: superficially he was very like Tim. He had the same blond hair and blue eyes, the same youthfully handsome face, a certain assurance about him that suggested he knew what he wanted and tried his damnedest to get it. Hadn't he just confirmed that? He had wanted to get to know her, and here she was talking to him as if he were an old friend.

"That's very flattering," she replied, keeping her tone light.

"It wasn't meant to be," he said seriously. "It was just a statement of fact. Where did you get those lovely golden eyes?" he demanded suddenly.

Eden laughed, a lighthearted carefree sound. She was

young, reasonably pretty, and Gary Nichols was very attractive. Suddenly the world seemed a little brighter. "From my grandfather, or so I've been told."

He frowned. "Don't you know?"

Her smile faded. "I never met him. My parents were divorced," she explained briefly. "Tell me, what do you do for a living that you have a Tuesday afternoon off?" she asked, changing the subject.

"You see before you the next great artist of the decade," he jokingly told her.

"I do?" she teased. "I don't remember ever seeing a Gary Nichols painting."

"Oh, you haven't. No, they're so rare and exclusive that anyone who has one keeps it firmly under lock and key."

"I see," she said, tongue in cheek. "You must be good."

Gary laughed. "Seriously, I am hoping for great things one day. I have an exhibition in a few months' time."

Eden was suitably impressed. "Then you *are* good. I'd like to see some of your work sometime."

"I'll have to remember that. 'Would you like to come up and see my paintings?'" he quipped. "So original," he added, grimacing. "Although there's a problem about that—I share a flat."

"Hard luck," she teased.

"What do you do? Or are you just over for a holiday?"

She sobered as she remembered all too clearly her reason for being in England. "Neither. I, er, I'm here visiting relatives."

"You're staying with them?" He sipped his coffee.

"I'm staying with—with Jason. He was a friend of my grandfather's," she explained at his sharp look. "Really," she added as she saw his look of speculation. "He's Jason Earle," she said desperately.

"He's taking out Isobel Morton, isn't he?"

Eden frowned. "You know about that?"

"Well, I should; it's in the newspapers this morning.
Here—" he pulled a crumpled edition out of his coat
pocket, spreading it out on the table "—see. The article's
about the death of David Morton, but it does mention that—
Hey, are you all right?" He noticed her pallor for the first
time.

"Yes, I—I'm fine." She hadn't realized her grandfather's
death would make the headlines. The newspaper Mrs. Gifford had brought in for her had remained untouched on the
table, and she wished now she had thought to look at it. Her
grandfather's death looked so stark printed there in black
and white, and it wasn't the sort of thing she would have
wanted to see for the first time in front of a stranger.
"Would you excuse me?" She stood up shakily, dashing to
the washroom that was nearby.

She had seen a picture of Jason and Isobel Morton in the
article, a picture of them together at some charity dinner
they had attended; and there had been another photograph,
one of her grandfather. He looked very much as she had
thought he would look, tall and thin, with a strong determination to his harsh face, his thick hair iron gray and very
distinguished. It was impossible to tell the color of his eyes,
but they looked a curiously clear color—tawny, Jason had
called them.

Her breakfast left her body with an aching wrench, although she felt much better when the sickness had passed.
She splashed cold water all over her face, refreshed if still
very pale. While she had been able to think of her grandfather as a romote figure in the background of her life, his
death hadn't meant that much to her; but seeing what he
had looked like made it a painful reality. She may not have
known him, but in the end he had cared enough about her
to provide for her.

Now she cried the tears that wouldn't come yesterday, cried for all the years wasted, years when she and her grandfather could have been close in their hearts if not in miles. She sobbed and sobbed, glad that no other women came into the room to interrupt her grief.

Finally she calmed, a curious peace coming over her as she came to a decision. She would stop fighting Jason about staying in England, would accept the gift her grandfather had made her, would stay here as he had obviously intended her to. The decision made, she made the necessary repairs to her makeup, a certain redness to her eyes the sole evidence of her grief by the time she had finished. Only someone with a discerning eye would know she had been crying at all.

Unfortunately, Gary had more than a discerning eye; he had an artist's critical gaze, and knew straightaway the tears she had shed. "Let's go," he said instantly as she rejoined him. "I've already paid the bill."

Eden followed him in a slight daze, not as collected as she had thought she was.

"What an idiot I am," Gary muttered almost to himself. "I should have realized.... You're the granddaughter who arrived from America yesterday."

Her eyes widened. "The newspaper mentioned me?"

"It mentions the whole family. God, I'm sorry. I really went in with both feet there." He sighed. "I should have known, should have connected— As soon as you said Jason Earle was a friend of your grandfather's I should have known. I'm really sorry."

"It's all right." She gave a rather wan smile. "Just reaction setting in, I think."

"I'm not surprised. It must have been a terrible experience for you, to arrive just too late! What an awful thing to happen."

"It was, rather," she admitted quietly. "Still—" she straightened her shoulders "—life has a way of turning out like that." As she was learning to her cost. And the repercussion of her grandfather's death was that Isobel Morton hated her, really hated her. But it didn't matter, couldn't matter, because no matter what the opposition she was going to take over her grandfather's business interests, would somehow contrive to continue with his success. Jason had said her grandfather had made provision for her inexperience, and so perhaps she wouldn't find it as difficult to carry out his work as she had at first thought.

"Are you feeling better now?" Gary looked down at her with concerned blue eyes.

"Much." She even managed another smile. "It never pays to bottle these things up. But I'll be fine now. I rarely cry about something a second time." Although death had never touched her before.

"But surely—"

"Would you mind if I left you now, Gary?" she cut in. "I'd like to go home—back to Jason's." She turned away, only to turn back again. "Thank you for the coffee," she murmured.

Gary put out a hand to stop her. "Let me drive you home."

"No! Really. I . . . I can get a taxi."

"I'll drive you," he insisted firmly, taking charge of her. "It's the least I can do."

She could imagine Jason's face if he saw her turn up with Gary! "I'd rather—"

"Let me, Eden. Please. I'd like to."

She couldn't resist the little-boy appeal in his eyes. "Okay. But I can't ask you in," she added hastily. "I'm only a guest there."

"I'll just drive you back and leave you at the door," he promised.

His car was parked outside his flat, ten minutes' walk away. He raised his eyebrows when she gave him the address, but made no comment. But the look was enough, telling her that Jason's house must stand in an exclusive area of London.

He came around to open the door for her once they reached the house. "Can I see you again?"

She shook her head. "I'm unsure of my plans."

"Please, Eden." His voice had lowered pleadingly. "I'd like to see you again."

"I don't think so."

"Say yes, Eden," he prompted. "Or at least give me your telephone number."

She bit her lip thoughtfully. He had been nice to her, that she couldn't deny. Besides, he was at least one friend in what had so far seemed a totally hostile country to her. "I may be moving from here soon; this is only a temporary measure."

"Surely Mr. Earle would be able to pass on where you've gone to."

"Okay." She handed him the slip of paper from her pocket on which she had written the telephone number down for herself. "But if Jason answers I couldn't guarantee his mood to you. He can be very surly." That was an understatement!

Gary grinned. "So I've read. I'll be polite, don't worry. But I'll leave it for a couple of days. You, er, you'll have a lot of things to do the next few days."

"Leave it until next week," she advised. "Maybe by then things will have fallen into some sort of order." Although with Jason around she doubted it!

She stood and waved to him as he drove off, aware of

having made a friend. The "things" he had referred to would consist mainly of attending the funeral. But she wouldn't cry, she knew she wouldn't; she was all cried out. And that would just convince Jason what a hard little bitch she was. If only he knew!

Before she had time to knock, the front door flew open with a crash and Jason stood in front of her, his face contorted with anger. He pulled her ruthlessly inside and slammed the door, dragging her into the privacy of his study before pushing her away from him.

"Where the hell have you been?" he demanded through gritted teeth.

Eden blinked dazedly. "I've been out. I told Mrs. Gifford—"

"That you were going to look at the shops," he finished grimly. "And yet you arrived back here with some man in tow."

"How do you know it wasn't a taxi?" Although she had to admit that the gold-and-black Mini hadn't looked anything like a taxi.

He eyed her suspiciously "Was it?"

"No," she admitted guiltily, looking down at the carpet, anywhere but into that lividly angry face.

"So, where did you pick him up?"

"At the park," she mumbled.

"You mean, you *did* pick him up?" Jason sounded incredulous.

"Well, I.... No. He—"

"He picked you up. My God! You don't waste time, do you?" His gaze swept over her with obvious disgust. "Here one day and already you've found a man to share your bed."

Color flooded her cheeks, cheeks that seconds ago had been deathly white. How dared he! How *dared* he! "*Another* man," she said with emphasis. "I already have an open invitation from you."

"You little—"

"Was I mistaken?" she asked with feigned innocence. "Last night you—"

"Shut up, you little bitch!" he ordered savagely. "Isobel is in the lounge. And you know damned well how possessive she's suddenly become of me."

"Oh, God ..." Eden groaned. Her desire to hit out at Jason hadn't included hurting the curiously vulnerable Isobel Morton. "Why didn't you tell me?" she demanded in a fierce whisper.

"I didn't think it was necessary," he muttered furiously. "You said you had no intention of hitting out at Isobel through me."

"And I still haven't," she hissed. "Not with someone like you involved. Gary is much more my type; he doesn't make a big thing about sleeping together."

"He just does it, I suppose," Jason scoffed.

"That's right." She glared at him defiantly. "Shouldn't you be getting back to your fiancée?" she sneered.

Those gray eyes kindled dangerously. "She is not my fiancée and never has been! And she's here to see you."

Eden couldn't hide her surprise. "She is?"

"Yes. She wants you to move in with her."

"But she said— Oh, I get it," Eden remarked scornfully. "She doesn't really want me living with her, but she doesn't want me staying here with you, either. Well, thanks, but no thanks. If you want me to move out of here I'll go to a hotel."

"I don't want you to move out, for God's sake!" he snapped. "Isobel just thought—"

"I'll bet she did," Eden said vehemently. "I'm not going! I refuse to go! I don't want to go and stay with *her*."

"I get the message, Eden," he drawled. "Don't protest

too much; I might get the impression that it's really because you don't want to leave me."

"Then you would be wrong. If your example just now of exploding simply because I came back with a man is anything to go by, I—"

"A man you admit you let pick you up," he cut in coldly. "Just what kind of girl are you?"

"I thought you had me all worked out, Jason. I'm a girl out for every cheap thrill I can get, even from someone I met only today in the park. With the exception of you, I don't even care who it is, as long as he's male. And I don't want to have to answer to you for my every move. I'd have more freedom at a hotel. I—"

"Shut up, girl!" He took her savagely by the shoulders, bending his head to grind lips down on hers in a gesture that was purely anger and owed nothing to passion. When he finally put her away from him she was dazedly silent. "That's one way of quieting you," he said with satisfaction.

"Jason...." All the fire had died out of her, his punishing kiss subduing her as nothing else could have done.

His eyes darkened. "Oh, God, Eden, you—"

"Jason? Jason, where are you?" Isobel Morton's husky voice called out to him. "Darling?"

Eden had stiffened at the first sound of that seductive voice, gathering her scattered defenses together with an effort. Why was it that Jason had the power to make her forget everything but him? She had forgotten Isobel Morton, forgotten everything but the feel of his lips on hers. "I think she wants you," she told him shakily.

"A second ago I thought *you* wanted me." He watched her with narrowed eyes.

"Oh!" she gasped at his bluntness, "You bigheaded—"

"There you are, darling." Isobel Morton came into the room. "And Eden, too."

Jason frowned at her, moving to her side. "You should have stayed in the other room. You know you aren't well."

In fact she didn't look well, her cheeks chalky white, her lipstick a vivid splash of color in her face, the brown eyes shadowed. She was still well-groomed, her clothes perfect, her hair styled in soft waves, and yet the recent bereavement seemed to have hit her hard.

Isobel smiled at him. "I was worried about you, darling. You seemed to have been gone such a long time. I didn't realize Eden was here."

"She arrived a few minutes ago." Jason turned her firmly back toward the lounge, seeing her seated before turning to face Eden.

Eden flinched at the warning in his eyes. Just what sort of person did he think she was? Did he think she was going to tell this woman who seemed to think she had some claim on him that only seconds ago he had been kissing her, that he had kissed her last night, too? Did he really think she would do a thing like that? This woman may have taken her father from her mother, but Eden certainly wouldn't do the same thing to her.

"How are you feeling now?" Eden asked her politely.

"Better, thank you," Isobel replied rather coolly. "I believe I was rather rude to you yesterday. I'm sorry."

Whatever Eden had expected from this woman, it had not been an apology. After all, she must be feeling very bitter still about the way David Morton had left his money.

"Jason tells me my behavior was atrocious," Isobel continued. "He was quite cross with me."

These words somehow took away the sincerity of the apology made only seconds earlier. Eden had no doubt that if Jason hadn't been "cross" with Isobel, no apology would have been forthcoming. "That's perfectly all right," she accepted distantly.

Anger flashed momentarily in those dark brown eyes before it was quickly masked. Isobel put her hand on Jason's thigh as he sat beside her on the sofa, smiling up at him. "He can be such a bear," she said, as if it didn't matter what mood he was in as long as he was with her.

Their relationship sickened Eden. No matter what Isobel Morton felt for Jason, and Eden doubted it was love, she knew he was not in love with this woman, being too much of a cynic ever to fall in love and so make himself vulnerable to any woman. Besides, he couldn't have been so familiar with Eden herself and be in love with Isobel.

"I can imagine," Eden said dryly, noting with satisfaction the involuntary tightening of Jason's mouth. "But you have no need to apologize; I understood perfectly." She understood that this woman hated her guts!

"There you are, darling." Isobel looked poutingly at Jason. "Now are you going to stop being so annoyed with me?"

He removed her hand from his thigh. "I'm not annoyed with you," he said impatiently. "And you had no need to make the apology right now. I merely told you to make one when you were feeling better. I didn't expect you to insist on coming here today."

"I didn't come here just for that," Isobel replied smoothly. "You must realize that Eden can't stay here with you any longer."

Eden stiffened. "But I—"

"You must see it won't do, Eden." Isobel looked at her with hard eyes. "You can't stay here alone with Jason. The press would make a meal out of information like that."

Eden's mouth twisted with bitter humor. "I can assure you I have no designs—"

"Eden and I have talked about it, Isobel," Jason cut in firmly, his tone brooking no further argument from her. "I think for the time being it would be better if she stayed here. I know this is hardly the time to discuss it, but once David's will comes into operation I'm going to need easy access to Eden."

Eden's eyes widened. "What on earth do you mean? What does...what does my grandfather's will have to do with you?"

"Quite a lot," he said tautly. "As you'll soon find out."

She frowned. "But I don't understand...."

"It's perfectly simple," Isobel Morton snapped. "Your grandfather has left you *almost* everything he possessed, but in his wisdom he has left it to you under the guidance of Jason."

Eden gulped. "You mean—"

"I mean that in a way Jason is now your guardian." Isobel glared at her with dislike.

CHAPTER SIX

"BUT HE CAN'T BE!" Eden gasped. "I have a mother and a stepfather. I can't just be put under the guardianship of a complete stranger!"

"I won't be that sort of guardian," Jason told her in a bored voice. "Although there are some aspects of your life that could use a little controlling."

She had no doubt which "aspects" he referred to. "Then what sort of guardian will you be?" she demanded to know, sitting on the edge of her seat in her agitation.

He shrugged. "A financial and business one. David has arranged things so that you will reap financial benefit—at my discretion, of course—but have to worry about none of the actual business involved. I will be taking care of that."

So this was what he had meant when he said provision had been made for her inexperience in all things financial! "I see." She bit her lip. "Could I contest that condition?" she asked, eyeing him defiantly.

His mouth was a grim angry line. "You could try, but I don't think it would get you very far. The will is pretty explicit."

"And you agreed to it?" she almost accused.

"Of course."

"Will I have no say in—in anything to do with my grandfather's business affairs?"

"You will be consulted, yes," he told her arrogantly.

"But the ultimate decisions will always lie with you?"

"Yes," he nodded, a gleam of satisfaction in the depths of his gray eyes.

She glared at him. "God, why couldn't he have chosen anyone but you!"

Isobel smiled with malicious pleasure. "I don't think you're a hit with Eden, darling," she taunted. "A female who dislikes you... quite a novelty," she mused.

Jason's grim unsmiling mouth and narrowed eyes were evidence of his anger at Eden's childish display of temper. And it had been childish, she knew that. Whatever else this man might be, and no matter what she thought of his moral conduct, he was a financial genius. Her grandfather had obviously known that, too.

And Isobel Morton was quite wrong about Eden's feelings toward Jason. She didn't dislike him; on the contrary, given the right circumstances she could like him altogether too much. Thank God these were nowhere near the right circumstances!

This afternoon she had made the decision to stay in England as her grandfather had wanted her to, but at the time she hadn't realized she would have to come into quite as much contact with Jason as his being her financial guardian would entail. Would she now be able to keep to her decision to stay?

"Eden hasn't yet learned that it isn't always prudent to show one's feelings of dislike quite so plainly," Jason drawled. "Her aversion to me has been obvious from the beginning, although there have been a couple of occasions when it wasn't quite so much in evidence." He looked challengingly at her.

Color flooded her cheeks, and she glanced meaningfully at Isobel Morton. But Jason's look egged her on to further insults. "I have disliked you since the first moment we met," she told him, "and I believe the feeling is mutual."

Turning to Isobel, she added, "So you see, Mrs. Morton, no matter what the press might like to think, I do not have designs on Jason."

"I should hope not," Isobel hissed. "When I mentioned the press I meant that they would perhaps think it odd that you aren't staying at your grandfather's house. I certainly didn't mean that Jason and you— The idea is ridiculous!" she said scornfully.

"Yes," Eden couldn't help the taunting smile she gave Jason. He didn't look in the least amused, increasing her own humor. "Utterly ridiculous," she agreed.

"Of course it is," the other woman dismissed the subject. "And call me 'Isobel'; 'Mrs. Morton' is much too formal."

"Isobel," Eden reluctantly acknowledged.

"Eden stays here." Jason took control again. "Where I can keep an eye on her."

Isobel flushed angrily. "I'm quite capable of doing that," she snapped, obviously not pleased about leaving them there together despite her denial a few seconds earlier.

"She's a little—high-strung," Jason drawled. "She needs a firm hand."

"I don't need any sort of hand!" Eden put in furiously. "And certainly not yours," she added insultingly.

"I disagree," he said coldly, his eyes glacial. "From what I've seen of your behavior so far, I think you need constant supervision."

"Day and night?" she challenged sweetly.

"If necessary," he said tightly.

"Darling," Isobel crooned, her hand back on his thigh in a possessive gesture, "stop shouting at the poor girl."

"I wasn't shouting," he bit out.

"Perhaps not," she soothed. "But you're both being very insulting to each other. I do think my suggestion that Eden move in with me is the only sensible thing to do."

"No!" Eden instantly refused.

"I don't think so, either." For once Jason sided with her. "You have enough to think about without having to worry about whose bed Eden might be occupying every time she's out of the house."

Eden went white. Saying things like that to her in private was one thing, but saying them in front of this woman, who was listening with obvious relish, was another. Before Jason could say anything else she had sprung up out of her chair, walked over to him with angry strides and swung her hand hard against his face. She didn't wait to see his reaction as she hurried out of the room, looking neither left nor right, intent only on getting away.

Jason caught up with her just as she had her foot on the first stair, swinging her around to face him. The marks of her hand stood out lividly red against the white-hot anger revealed in his face. "I warned you about ever hitting me," he reminded her with slow-burning anger. "I warned you—"

"Yes, you warned me!" She flicked her head back defiantly. "You also told me what to expect if I did." To her shame, hot angry tears threatened to blind her. She blinked and they cascaded down her cheeks, her bottom lip trembling. "Well, you go ahead and hit me back; it's only what I would expect from a man like you."

"I'm sorry to disappoint you," he ground out coldly, unmoved by her tears, "but your punishment will have to wait until later. Perhaps that's what you're hoping for; maybe what you really want is what I said would follow my retaliation."

"If you ever kiss me again I think I'll be sick," she choked.

He twisted her arm behind her back, the movement bringing her close to the lean length of his body. "I've never been able to understand how a man can hit out and strike a woman, but with you I'm coming dangerously close to it. Don't try your luck too far, Eden. My restraint might not hold out much longer.''

"What do I care?'' She struggled out of his grasp. "You enjoy intimidating me. Well, that slap was just to show you that I won't stand for it.'' Her eyes sparkled like gold as she put up a hand to wipe away all traces of tears. "You can say what you want to me in private, but I—I won't be humiliated in front of that woman.''

"May I remind you that you started the backbiting in front of Isobel? I was being remarkably restrained, considering I had just caught you sneaking back to the house after spending the afternoon God knows where with someone you let pick you up.''

"We spent the afternoon talking in a café,'' she told him in a choked whisper. "I—I needed someone to talk to.''

"Then why the hell didn't you talk to me?''

"You weren't here! You'd gone to work, remember?''

"And so you let yourself be picked up by some— Did you sleep with him?'' he demanded to know.

Her mouth began to tremble again. "No, I didn't! I only met him today, and—''

"And you usually wait until at least the second date,'' he finished tauntingly. "I suppose that makes you feel better.''

"I hate you, Jason Earle!'' She swung away from him, and this time he made no effort to stop her.

The decision she had made in the café now seemed to be one she couldn't keep. If she stayed in England and accepted her inheritance, she would have to see more of Jason than was good for her. *He* wasn't good for her. He had a twisted mind that distorted everything she did, made her even suspect her own actions.

There had been nothing sordid or disgusting about her talking to Gary that afternoon. Okay, so she accepted that perhaps it wasn't quite the proper thing for a well-brought-up young lady to speak to a complete stranger in that way, but it certainly didn't make her the Queen of Tramps, either. Gary had been very nice, with nothing lecherous about him, although she would never get Jason to believe that. He didn't want to believe it, preferring to keep his bad impression of her.

Admittedly the two of them had got off to a bad start, had seemed to strike sparks off each other ever since, but she had never known anyone to dislike her as much as he did. He seemed to delight in thinking the worst of her, seemed to enjoy insulting her with what he thought to be the truth about her morals.

She sat in the window seat in her bedroom, gazing down at the garden at the front of the house. Jason's personalized Jaguar stood in the driveway, evidence that he and Isobel Morton were still downstairs.

The telephone by her bed began to ring, making her jump nervously. "Yes?" she asked shakily.

"Your boyfriend is on the line," came Jason's terse comment. "Feel like talking to him?"

Gary? But she had asked him not to call until next week. Oh, well, she didn't care what his reason was, she would just be glad to talk to someone who didn't think she was the local prostitute. "Yes, I'll talk to him," she said breathlessly.

There was a click, and then she could hear the crackly sound of the telephone line. "Eden? Eden, are you there?"

It wasn't Gary at all; this voice was definitely American. "Tim?" she asked uncertainly.

"Who else were you expecting it to be, honey?" he teased.

"Don't you start," she snapped, and then regretted it.
"Sorry, Tim. I'm a bit tense at the moment."

"I'm not surprised. I'm really sorry about your grandfather, even more so because I tried to stop you from going
over there. Did you get to meet him before—"

"No. How did you know about it?"

"It was in the newspapers over here. I called Jason on the
off chance that he could tell me your telephone number,
and he said you're staying with him. So you didn't get to see
your grandfather?"

"He died before I got here," she said dully.

"That's too bad. But I suppose you'll be coming home
now?" he asked hopefully. "I'm sorry about your grandfather, and it's tragic that you should have got there too
late, but I'm missing you so much, Eden. When are you
coming home?"

"Not for a while." She explained the conditions of her
grandfather's will to him.

"That's a strange thing for him to have done." She could
hear the puzzlement in his voice. "What if you had been
married? I'm sure your husband wouldn't have liked you to
have to rely on Jason in that way."

"He wouldn't have any choice."

Tim gave a short laugh. "Poor Eden. It seems your
grandfather didn't trust women in business."

"I guess not," she agreed ruefully.

"How about marrying me? I couldn't give a damn about
Jason's being in charge over there."

"Only because you have so much money of your own."

"Surely that makes me ideal husband material for you,"
he said eagerly.

"I thought you had changed your mind about marrying
me?"

"You angered me, Eden," he sighed. "You're the first

girl I've ever asked to marry me, and I—it came as something of a shock when you turned me down. Blame the anger on my conceit. I just didn't think you would say no.''

No girl in her right mind would have done, not with Tim heir to all those millions of dollars. Besides which, he was a good-looking young man. "Maybe you caught me at a bad time, Tim. Jason had just sprung the idea of seeing my grandfather on me.''

"You also said you wanted to travel," he reminded her.

"Not anymore," she answered with a shudder. "You were right, Tim; it's very lonely being in a country where no one is your friend." Her voice broke with emotion. "Everyone thinks I'm an unwanted nuisance.''

"Then come home," he repeated.

"I can't," she told him ruefully, just longing for the sight of a friendly face. "At least, not yet. I feel I would be letting my grandfather down if I left now.''

"Then how about if I come over to you? Dad's sending me to Germany on business for a few days, and I could come on to England from there.''

"That would be lovely," she agreed enthusiastically. "I'm not finding it all that easy to cope with the loneliness— and hostility." Or Jason Earle, for that matter!

"How come you're staying with Jason?" Tim asked, almost as if he could read her thoughts. But that was silly; he couldn't possibly know the effect Jason was having on her. "I persuaded Claire to give me Jason's telephone number," he continued, "just in the hope that he might be able to tell me where I could reach you. I couldn't have been more shocked when he said you were staying with him.''

"Even if I wanted to stay with Isobel Morton, which I don't, I don't really think she is in any state to entertain guests," she prevaricated. So Claire Channing knew Jason's home number!

"But you're a member of the family, not a guest!"

"Not to her, Tim. Besides, the house is hers now."

"But staying with Jason isn't a very good arrangement, either." He gave an abrupt laugh. "I daren't tell Claire; she would go insane with jealousy."

"There's nothing like that between us!" she snapped.

"I didn't for one minute— There isn't, is there?" he asked suspiciously.

"I've just said there isn't!"

"It was the way you said it, sort of on the defensive. I know Jason, and if he can seduce my hardened big sister into his bed then he could get a baby like you there with hardly any effort at all."

"Except that I may not be willing to share his bed. Really, Tim, if I can deny you, someone I'm very fond of, I'm hardly likely to give in to someone I don't even like."

"Mmm, I suppose not." But he didn't sound too sure. "Nevertheless, I'll get to England as soon as I can. Will you still be at Jason's?"

Eden sighed. "No doubt about it. Jason tells me he wants to keep a fatherly eye on me, ward off all the predatory males—or was it *warn* off? He thinks I'm a man trap," she explained with a laugh.

"*You* are? My distant Eden? For an astute man, he has you read all wrong."

"He hasn't if you consider that's the impression I've been trying to give him."

"But why? Never mind—we can talk about it when I get there. I'm missing you, honey," he added huskily.

"I'm missing you, too." If only for his pleasant companionship. There had been little of that for her so far in England. "Call me from Germany and I'll meet your flight in."

"I'll do that. See you soon, honey." And he rang off.

Somehow she must have lain down on the bed and fallen asleep, because the next thing she knew she was waking up and it was pitch-black outside. What on earth could the time be? She sat up in a panic, pushing back the blanket covering her to look at the slender gold watch on her wrist. Ten-thirty! God, she had been asleep for more than four hours. The rumblings of her stomach told her that she had missed out completely on dinner, and after the meager lunch she had enjoyed in the park, she was feeling decidedly hungry.

By the lateness of the hour she presumed Mrs. Gifford would have retired for the night; Jason seemed to dismiss her after dinner. Dinner! Goodness, she could do with a hot meal, anything to fill the hunger gnawing at her body. The blanket pulled over her showed that the housekeeper hadn't forgotten her, but Mrs. Gifford had no doubt considered she needed sleep more than food. At the time she had probably been right—last night's sleep hadn't been very restful—but now hunger was the predominant feeling.

Jason would most likely still be with Isobel Morton, although she would check on that before she raided the kitchen. If he wasn't in his study then he was out. She looked down at her crumpled lemon denims and crushed sweater, debating whether or not it was worth changing them, just in case Jason was home. The clothes were really too creased to be viewed by anyone but herself.

In the end she decided against it, still feeling slightly sleepy. Besides, it was late. There was a light on in the hall-way, but otherwise the house was in darkness. Good—that meant she could have something to eat without fear of being disturbed. There seemed to be plenty of eggs and salad stuff in the fridge, and so she made herself a cheese omelet with salad, not wanting anything too heavy at this time of night.

She had just finished the last of her meal and was halfway through her glass of milk when the kitchen door swung open and Jason Earle walked in, the debris of a meal on the tray in his hand. He raised his eyebrows at her seated at the kitchen table, the only light in the room the one over the stove. Eden hadn't wanted him to know she was in there if he happened to come home while she was eating; now it appeared he had been in the house all the time. But he definitely hadn't been in his study, so where had he been?

"I was working at the desk in my room," he supplied the answer to her unasked question. "I just looked in on you to see if you were ready for anything to eat yet." He put the tray down, leaning back against one of the kitchen cabinets to look at her, making no effort to switch on the main light.

He was dressed much less formally than she had ever seen him, the faded denims resting low down on his hips and molded to his powerful thighs. His navy blue shirt was partly unbuttoned, the dark hair in evidence there curled together in tiny knots, as if he had been unconsciously tangling it with his fingers.

His appearance had the effect of making Eden tongue-tied. "I, er, I was hungry," she stated the obvious in her nervousness. "I...I hope Mrs. Gifford won't, um, mind my coming in here."

"I would doubt it; she left at six. It's her night off, and I always get my own meal on a Tuesday."

Eden frowned. If the housekeeper had left at six, then she had left before Eden had fallen asleep. Then who— "It was you," she blurted out.

"What was me?" he asked tolerantly, as if he were dealing with a backward child.

She looked at him dazedly. "You put the blanket over me."

"So?"

"So I...I...." Weren't you at your most vulnerable when you were asleep? She didn't like the idea of this man seeing her even slightly vulnerable!

Jason gave a taunting smile, his gray eyes openly mocking her. "You were perfectly decent, I can assure you. In fact, you looked rather endearing. You were sucking your thumb."

"Oh." Bright red color flooded her cheeks. She always resorted to this habit in sleep when she was worried or upset.

Gray eyes hardened as they swept over the untidiness of her clothes and the ruffled beauty of her short golden hair. "I was more worried about the pillow you were clutching so frantically to you," he said slowly, watching her closely. "Who were you imagining it was, Eden?" he asked huskily. "Who was the man in your arms?"

"Well, it certainly wasn't you," she snapped.

He moved to pull her to her feet, holding her immovable against him. "Wasn't it?"

"No!" She wrenched her gaze away from the mesmerizing effect of eyes gone suddenly black.

"Tim, perhaps?" he asked, his voice dangerously soft. "Or was it the new boyfriend?"

"Whoever it was, it has nothing to do with you!" She wished she felt as brave as her words sounded! "My dreams—"

"Fantasies," he corrected suggestively. "From the smile on your face it was a fantasy."

"Oh." Again she blushed, as he had no doubt intended she should. "My fantasies, then," she said crossly, "are my own affair."

"Not if I was in them," he murmured throatily. "I've always believed in making fantasy reality."

"I'm sure you have," she retorted, wishing he wouldn't

hold her quite so tightly, wishing he wouldn't hold her at all! "But you weren't in my mind. Tim was," she added defiantly.

"Liar," he said throatily. "Aren't you going to tempt me with your forbidden fruit, Eden?"

She held on to her senses with effort, feeling seduced by the intimacy of his voice. She made her next words as chilly as possible in the hope of stopping this attack on her already crumbling defenses by his practiced seduction. "I realize that Isobel isn't in the mood to accommodate your undoubtable sex drive," she said scathingly. "But I hardly think that reason enough for you to take me to your bed instead."

To her chagrin, her words didn't seem to anger him; in fact, they seemed to amuse him. "When my sex drive needs accommodating," he mocked, "I go to women who can cause me much less trouble than you. Yes, women like Claire," he put in before she said it. "But I don't want you to *accommodate* me. I want to make love to you, and I want you to make love to me."

Eden gulped. "Make love to you...?"

"Yes." His lips traveled lightly over her throat. "Too many women think that simply by being there they've done their bit." He laughed. "But you won't be like that; you'll know how to please me as I please you."

"No!" She pushed away from him, but with little effect. "Please stop it. You—you've punished me enough."

His eyes glittered as he looked fiercely down at her. "Ah, yes." His brow cleared. "For your slap this afternoon," he went on, touching his injured cheek. "I have to admit to forgetting all about it. I'd also forgotten that you said if I kissed you again you would be sick." His smile mocked. "The feeling I've aroused is far from nausea."

"You've angered me—"

"It isn't anger, either." He laughed at her outraged face. "Why is it women are afraid to show passion, to share it? I'd be aroused just by seeing your eyes glazed with passion for me—as they are now. And I am aroused, Eden."

"I...I know," she whispered. She had been aware of his rising desire for some time now. "But I—I can't! I—my grandfather hasn't even been buried yet!" she cried in desperation.

Instantly she was set free, and Jason stood several feet away from her. He turned back to look at her when he had himself under control. "Was that really the reason you stopped me?" he demanded harshly. "Or was it something else?"

"I...it just doesn't seem right in the circumstances." Surely she was allowed to lie at such a time!

If he had thought it was simply a case of inexperience, he would have tried to seduce her into his bed anyway—and no doubt he would have succeeded. It might have been worth it just to see his face when he realized he had taken a virgin.

Was she crazy? Of course it wouldn't have been worth it! She may be old-fashioned, but the man she married would be her first and only lover, on that she was determined. Not that Jason Earle would ever believe that without proof; and as he wasn't, and never could be, the man she intended marrying, he would never be given the opportunity to find out. He could think what he liked about her; no matter what she told him, he didn't believe her.

"You're probably right," he said now. "I'll remind you of tonight at a later date."

"Yes. I, er, I thought you would be dining with Isobel tonight," she changed the subject, moving to the sink to wash her plate and glass before putting them away.

"I checked on you before I drove Isobel home, and since you were asleep I didn't think I should leave you alone in the house any longer than necessary. I thought you might wake up and wonder where everyone was, so I came straight back."

"That was nice of you. It was also thoughtful of you to put the blanket over me; it had turned quite cold while I was asleep."

Jason smiled, only a trace of his usual sarcasm in evidence. "I can be thoughtful on occasion."

Eden grinned. "All the other women in your life seem to think so." Now that any immediate danger had passed, she didn't mind indulging in a little lighthearted teasing with him.

Those gray eyes were seductively soft. "Are you one of the women in my life?"

"I remember you once told me I wasn't a woman."

"Or experienced," he derided her. "How wrong could I be!"

"Jason . . . ."

"Mmm?"

"Oh—nothing." She gave him a bright smile. "Did you decide where I'm to stay?"

"*I* didn't, *you* did. You told me you wouldn't go with Isobel."

"So I stay here?"

He nodded. "You stay here. *Do* you think I'm old enough to be your father?" he asked suddenly.

She grinned, surprised that he had remembered her making that remark. "That rankled, hmm?"

"A little," he admitted ruefully. "Make me a coffee, Eden."

"Please," she prompted.

"Make me a coffee, Eden—please," he said mockingly.

"That wasn't quite what I had in mind. You still managed to make it sound like an order."

He laughed. "It was meant to."

"You're impossible!"

"Not impossible, Eden. I think I could be managed by the right woman."

"You just haven't met her yet," she taunted.

"I may have done," he told her abruptly.

"Then it can't be Isobel." He could never behave with other women the way he did if he were in love with Isobel Morton.

"I already told you it wasn't. The coffee, Eden," he reminded her.

"You're very single-minded," she said crossly, doing as he suggested and preparing coffee for them both. She had been finding the conversation very interesting, damn him. "I suppose you are old enough to be my father," she told him bitchily. "I presume you weren't a virgin at sixteen?"

"Do they call men 'virgins'?" he mused.

"I think so. I'm not sure."

"They probably do." He sipped his coffee, seated on a bar stool. "I wasn't a virgin." He grimaced as he said it. "It just doesn't sound right in reference to a man. I prefer to say I 'entered manhood.' And I did that on my sixteenth birthday."

She wasn't embarrassed by the conversation, just intrigued to think of Jason as a naive sixteen-year-old. "Do you think it's the same for a man—the first time is always the best and most important?"

"Hell, no!" he laughed. "It was a disaster. When I say I remember it, I don't mean it is a good memory. I blush just to think of it. I fumbled my way through it like the novice I was. She couldn't have got anything out of it at all."

"She got your virginity," Eden put in quietly.

"No great prize, I can tell you. But she was very beautiful, my art teacher, I remember that."

"She would have to be."

"Oh?"

"Mmm. I'm sure you were just as arrogant and demanding of perfection even then."

He laughed. "Arrogant? And demanding of perfection? Whatever gave you that idea?"

"You did. The first time we met you looked down your arrogant nose at me, and you've been doing it ever since."

Jason shook his head, still smiling, completely relaxed. "Your imagination, Eden. Or a guilt complex, I'm not sure which. I know you were damned rude to me at that first meeting. So—" his voice hardened "—was the first time good for you?"

Eden evaded his eyes as the two of them sat opposite each other at the table. "Well, I—"

"I don't see how it can possibly be the best," he said thoughtfully. "The most memorable, maybe, but surely not the best. I think the giving and receiving of absolute pleasure can come only with familiarity."

"I thought familiarity bred contempt?" she teased, glad not to have to answer his previous question.

"It can, especially in bed, but it's also necessary for perfect lovemaking."

"Jason, have you—" she ran the tip of her finger around the rim of her coffee mug, watching the movement and not him "—have you ever taken a virgin?"

"Never," he answered instantly.

Her eyes widened. "Never?"

He shook his head. "Sleeping with a woman is one thing, taking that away from her is another."

She forced a light laugh. "Goodness, how serious we've become!"

"The lateness of the hour and the intimacy of the situation, no doubt," Jason drawled, once again the arrogant tormentor of their first meeting. "I suggest we go to bed—for the moment in our respective bedrooms," he added mockingly as color flooded her cheeks.

"For the moment . . . ?"

"You did make me a half promise, Eden, one I intend keeping you to."

"But . . . but Isobel—"

"Has the idea that she would like to become my wife. It's just a feeling of insecurity; she leaned on David a lot despite his illness. When she gets over that she'll get over the idea of being my wife, I hope; because I have no intention of marrying her."

"But the newspapers—"

"Exaggerate. Just forget about Isobel," he instructed coldly. "Leave her to me."

"Gladly," she grimaced.

"Eden . . ." he groaned. "God, I've wanted you almost from the first moment I saw you."

"You—you have?"

"Mmm," he nodded. "If you weren't David's grand-daughter I would have done something about it by now."

"And the fact that I am his granddaughter?"

He shrugged. "It makes it a little difficult. But it will all work out in the end. Let's get to bed now; this can be talked out at a later date."

She intended being long gone before anything could come of tonight's conversation. But he could go on think-ing what he liked for the moment; time enough later on to let him know there could never be anything between them.

CHAPTER SEVEN

EDEN GULPED HER COFFEE DOWN so fast that she burned the inside of her mouth. She grimaced with pain, looking up to find Jason watching her over the top of his newspaper as he ate his breakfast at a leisurely pace. She gave him a harassed smile before gulping down yet more coffee.

"Are you in a hurry, by any chance?" he asked tauntingly.

"Yes," she answered unnecessarily.

Jason frowned at her haste. "Calm down, for God's sake! You're giving me indigestion."

"Sorry," she mumbled. "Anyway, I'm going now. Excuse me." She stood up.

He put out a hand to catch her wrist in a viselike grip. "Where are you going? The funeral—"

"Isn't until this afternoon." She tried to prize his fingers loose, but he wouldn't be moved. "Don't worry, I'll be back before then."

His eyes narrowed to steely slits. "Where are you going?" he repeated in a voice that demanded an answer.

"I just told you, I'm going out. Ouch!" she cried as his fingers tightened. "That hurt." She gave him a pouting look.

"It was meant to," he said unconcernedly. "Now that we've ascertained you're going out, all I want to know is where it is you're going in such a hurry."

"I, er, I'm meeting someone."

"Your young lover?"

"I don't have a lover, young or otherwise," she snapped.

"I gather the last part of that statement applies to me," he remarked dryly. "I'm the 'otherwise'," he explained at her puzzlement. "Old."

"You aren't old," she protested vehemently. "You—"

He grinned. "I'm not?"

She realized, too late, that she had walked into the trap he had set for her. "Well...not much," she amended.

"Cheeky!"

"Let me go, Jason," she pleaded. "I'll be late."

"He can wait for you. I'm going to claim a kiss first, and make it a good one, otherwise you'll be even later getting out."

She tried to still her suddenly ragged breathing. "Jason, please. He's expecting me and he...he won't wait."

"I would," he said throatily, his gaze resting intimately on her parted lips. "I'm waiting now."

"Jason, no!" She looked frantically around her for help, wishing Mrs. Gifford would come in and clear away the breakfast things. But she knew she wouldn't; the housekeeper always waited until they had left the room before entering.

"Jason, yes," he corrected softly. "I've been very patient, Eden. I haven't once tried to pressure you, even though you know you're driving me mad parading around the house in those tight denims of yours, every delicious curve clearly outlined."

"Jason...." She could feel herself weakening, his hand on her wrist having the seducing effect his touch usually had on her.

"I'm asking only for one kiss. I'm sure your young friend will ask for more, even if you aren't prepared to give it at the moment."

"Tim wouldn't—"

"Tim?" he echoed sharply. "You mean Tim Channing?"

"Yes," she admitted reluctantly.

His loverlike attitude had faded, a suspicious anger taking its place. "What does he have to do with your going out?" he demanded.

"I'm just on my way to meet him." She couldn't look at Jason, sensing his fury by the leashed tension in his body. "At the airport," she added lamely.

"He's coming *here*?"

She shook her head. "Not here. He's staying at a hotel."

"But he is coming to England?"

"Yes. He, er, he was in Germany on business and so—"

"How long have you known he was coming here?" he asked coldly.

"He telephoned yesterday and told me what time he would be arriving. You were at Isobel's, and I—I suppose I forgot to mention it last night."

"That doesn't answer my question," Jason said harshly. "I asked how long you've known about his coming to England."

"I. . . ."

"The truth, Eden!"

"Well, he—he did mention it on Tuesday." Although later events had temporarily put it out of her mind.

"Tuesday!" Jason echoed. "My God, that was the night— Just how many men can you cope with at one time? When Tim arrives you'll have three of us dangling on a bit of string, and that's just in England. I'm sure there must be others in the States."

"Oh, hundreds," she agreed flippantly, his accusations angering her as usual, their truce of the past two days completely disappearing. "I've always found safety in numbers. Although Tim wants to marry me," she told him defiantly.

His eyes narrowed. "He obviously doesn't realize what you are."

"He knows exactly what I am," Eden said truthfully. Tim knew her to be a friendly but certainly not promiscuous young woman.

"Then he must be insane to think of taking you on. He'll never control you."

"Have you never heard of making someone want something so badly that he's prepared to do anything to get it?" she asked with false bravado, stung by his obvious contempt. "Well, that's what I'm doing to Tim."

"Holding out on him, hmm? And it's working." He shook his head disgustedly.

"Yes." She gave him a triumphant smile. "It's working very well."

"So that was the reason you refused his proposal the first time. It was all part of the plan, wasn't it?" he said scornfully.

"Yes," she agreed dully, all the fight suddenly gone out of her. "It was all part of the plan. I should be Mrs. Tim Channing before the end of the year."

"Like hell you will!" Jason bit out forcefully.

"And just how do you intend stopping me? By telling Tim that I'm a tramp, that even you nearly had me? He wouldn't believe you, Jason," she smiled. "I've behaved in exemplary fashion with Tim. He would just think you had sour grapes because you didn't get anywhere with me. You have a reputation, you see—one that doesn't bear close inspection."

He wrenched her chin up, his fingers pressing painfully into her delicate skin. "Yours bears even less inspection," he ground out.

"I doubt you would find anyone, over here or in the States, to confirm your opinion of me. I've been very discreet," she told him tauntingly. "Yes, very discreet."

"You little bitch!" His face was an ugly mask.

She shrugged uncaringly. "I'll just add that to the list of other insults you've already given me; one more doesn't make any difference. I have to go now—I mustn't keep Tim waiting. I'll see you later."

"Invite him to stay here."

Eden turned to look at his rigid back. "Invite him here?"

He turned, his eyes glacial, a sneer on his lips. "Yes. His sister is a friend of mine, and it would look rude if he stayed at a hotel."

"I wouldn't have thought your friendship with Claire was something you would want Isobel to find out about—not in her vulnerable state."

"Tim will be your guest, not mine."

"How convenient for you."

"Yes," he said tightly. "I'll have Mrs. Gifford prepare a room for him."

"Not near mine, I hope," she said meaningfully. "I wouldn't like to give in to temptation."

"If you feel tempted, my room is just up from yours," he said abruptly.

"You . . . you still want me?"

"Well, let's just say I wouldn't turn you away," he drawled.

Eden's head rose haughtily. "I'll bear that in mind. And I'll give Tim your invitation. He can make up his own mind."

"Oh, he'll come," Jason said with certainty. "He won't refuse the opportunity of seeing more of you—and I didn't mean that literally," he added disgustedly.

She couldn't help laughing at his expression. "I think

you enjoy seeing me as some sort of scarlet woman," she smiled.

His expression remained grim. "I don't enjoy it at all. You look so innocent with that cap of golden hair and those wide innocent eyes." He shook his head. "But the body is a dead giveaway." His assessing gaze made her feel uncomfortable. "A dead giveaway," he murmured as if to himself.

Eden made a hurried goodbye, anxious to escape before he became any more familiar—or insulting. Their hostility was back with a vengeance!

She almost missed Tim at the airport; she was ten minutes late and apparently his flight had landed on time. He was just leaving as she rushed into the terminal.

She launched herself into his open arms. "Oh, Tim!" she choked, tears of happiness welling up into her eyes. "It's so good to see you."

He laughed exultantly at her undisguised enthusiasm. "So I gathered!" He claimed a lengthy kiss, uncaring of the people milling around them. "Mmm ... if being away from me for a few days has this effect on you, you'll have to do it more often."

She laughed happily, putting her arm around his waist as his rested on her shoulders. "Let's get out of here," she suggested as yet another person pushed passed them.

"Suits me," he grinned down at her. "Did Jason let you borrow his car?"

"I didn't think to ask him." Coolness entered her voice at the mention of Jason. "We can easily get a taxi. I saw lots of them outside when I came in."

"How is Jason?" Tim asked once they had attained their taxi and were on their way to London. "I have to ask or Claire won't be very pleased when I get back."

"You can see for yourself; you're expected to stay," she told him carelessly.

He raised his eyebrows. "At Jason's?"

She shrugged. "Where else?"

"Don't you want me to stay there?" He had gauged her mood and misunderstood it.

"Oh, yes," she said instantly. "More than anything."

"You still don't like him, do you," Tim commented, shaking his head.

Like him! Of course she didn't like him, she *loved* him. And that frightened her. How could she possibly have fallen in love with someone who had the opinion of her that Jason had? And yet she had; she had known it Tuesday night when they had talked together so intimately, had know it and feared it.

Jason didn't even like her; he desired her, but he didn't like her. All this time she had wondered why she couldn't fall in love with Tim or any of the other men she had dated the past few years, and now she knew the reason. It was her fate to fall for a heartless devil of a man called Jason Earle, a man who made no secret of his derision concerning marriage.

"No, I don't like him," she answered truthfully.

"And Isobel Morton, what's she like?"

"Beautiful, sophisticated, very self-assured."

"I suppose Jason sees a lot of her."

"Yes," Eden said abruptly, suddenly finding the idea of Jason being with Isobel Morton totally repugnant.

"How's the guardianship going?"

"It hasn't started yet," she answered with a grimace. "Jason thought it best to wait until after the funeral. But my mother was furious about that condition." Although it hadn't made her want Eden to refuse the inheritance. Angela considered that the money was the least David Morton could do for his granddaughter.

They got out of the taxi as it stopped outside Jason's

house. "Mmm, very impressive," Tim murmured as they entered the lounge. "But no more than I would expect for Jason."

"I suppose not," she agreed. "Sit down and we'll have a cup of coffee." She rang for Mrs. Gifford.

"Not tea?" Tim teased.

She laughed. "Not tea. They haven't persuaded me to drink it at all hours of the day just yet, although if I stay here much longer it will probably come to that."

"And will you be staying here much longer?"

"I'm not sure. Jason says— Ah, Mrs. Gifford." She smiled at the housekeeper. "This is Mr. Channing. Did Mr. Earle explain about him?"

"He did." The housekeeper gave a shy smile. "I've had a room prepared for you, Mr. Channing."

Tim had stood up at the woman's entrance, charming her with his most endearing smile. "Thank you," he said softly. "You're very kind."

She flushed with pleasure. "Not at all, sir. You're most welcome here."

"Could we possibly have coffee, Mrs. Gifford?" Eden asked persuasively, knowing that the preparation of Tim's room would have already put the poor woman's routine out completely.

"But of course, Miss Shaw," she answered as if there had never been any doubt of it.

"You were saying," Tim prompted once they were alone again. "Jason says...?"

"He said it could be a few months before everything is sorted out."

"But do you have to stay that long? It doesn't sound to me as if there's anything for you to do here."

Eden frowned. "I just don't want to leave yet. It's been a difficult week."

He put his hand over hers. "I'm sure it has."

"How did your business in Germany go?"

He shrugged. "It seemed okay to me, but no doubt it won't suit the parents." Tim was having to work his way up from the bottom of the family business—his mother's decision—and he didn't always find it easy satisfying his parents.

"Tim...." She hesitated. "Tim, this morning I told Jason—I told him I intended becoming your wife before the end of the year." She had to come clean, just in case Jason chose to tell Tim himself.

His face lighted up with pleasure. "You did?" he said eagerly. "Why, that's just—"

"I didn't mean it, Tim," she told him quietly.

"You didn't?" He frowned. "Then why...? Oh, no," he groaned. "Not another one."

She flushed. "Another what?"

"You've fallen for him, too, haven't you," he said resignedly.

"No!" she denied sharply. "I told you, I don't like—"

"You've fallen for him," he insisted. "I know the signs, remember?" He sighed. "What is it about him that attracts all the women? Oh, I know he's good-looking, has money; but then, without being conceited, I think I have both those things, too. Just why is it that he gets all the women?"

"Perhaps it's his elusiveness." She shrugged. "I don't know."

"Elusiveness." He chewed the word around. "You mean that if I suddenly started playing hard to get you might change your mind about me?"

"No." She gave a wan smile. "That isn't what I meant. Jason's elusiveness is mental, not physical. He isn't averse to sleeping with women, that much is obvious, but no woman gets to know his mind, the person behind the body;

and if you don't have that, then you don't have the man. When Drew met him he said Jason reminded him of an iceberg, at least eighty percent of him below the surface. It's that eighty percent that's the important part of him, the part he lets no one near.''

"No one?"

"I don't think so. It would make him vulnerable, you see, and Jason isn't a man who likes to feel vulnerable."

"You seem to have got to know him pretty well.'' Tim watched her with narrowed eyes.

"I told you—" she fidgeted with the seam of her denims "—eighty percent of him is below the surface."

"You sound as if you've penetrated at least forty percent of that. Given time you could even break down the whole hundred percent."

"Don't be silly, Tim." She avoided his probing look.

"I'm not being silly. Why did you tell him you intend marrying me if it wasn't some sort of defense? Has he been making passes at you?"

"No!"

"Liar!" he chided softly. "I told you, I know all the signs."

"Just because I...just because I find him attractive doesn't mean he feels the same way about me,'' she told him protestingly.

"You wouldn't need to be on the defensive if he didn't. Jason goes in for affairs and you don't, so you've given him the impression there's someone else."

"You're wrong, Tim." She gave a bitter laugh. "So very wrong. I didn't tell him that as a defense, I told him...." Somehow she didn't want to tell Tim of Jason's biased opinion of her. "Well, perhaps I did," she amended. "The man is completely without morals."

"I already knew that. When it involved only my sister I didn't care, but—"

"I don't think she would be pleased to hear that," Eden interrupted teasingly.

"She's old enough to know better than to make a fool of herself over someone like him, but she still chooses to see him."

"She doesn't choose to, Tim; she's in love with him." As Eden herself was!

"Then more fool her," he dismissed his sister callously. "And you, too, if you feel the same way. To have an affair with him you have to be removed emotionally, wanting only the physical."

"Maybe you're right."

"I am right," he said firmly. "And if you take my advice you'll keep up the pretense of becoming my wife. You never know," he grinned. "I might be able to make you agree to its becoming a reality."

"Tim, I wish you wouldn't—"

Mrs. Gifford came into the room after a brief knock, putting a laden tray down on the coffee table. "I've put some cakes on there, as well. I'm sure you must be hungry, Mr. Channing."

"Thank you." Once again he gave her his charming smile. "The food on airplanes is always atrocious."

The housekeeper smiled at him in return before leaving the room. "Behave yourself, Tim," Eden laughed. "Stop charming Jason's staff."

"I think she likes me." He bit into one of the buttered scones.

"I'm sure she does. Tim, I—"

This time someone entered the room without knocking, and Eden didn't need to look up to know it was the master of the house. She had assumed Jason was visiting Isobel, but once again she was wrong.

Tim stood up almost guiltily, at once in awe of the older man. "Jason," he said by way of greeting. "Very nice of you to invite me to stay," he added gruffly.

"Wasn't it?" Jason returned dryly. "I'll have some coffee, too, Eden. Mrs. Gifford said she had put three cups on the tray."

Eden had noticed the extra cup but had just thought it to be a mistake on the part of the housekeeper. It had never occurred to her that Jason would join them. She handed him the requested coffee without a word.

"Have I interrupted anything?" Jason asked at their continued silence.

He didn't look as if he particularly cared if he had! "No," Eden told him in a stilted voice.

"We were just talking about the wedding," Tim said casually.

Eden and Jason both gave him sharp looks, but Jason was the first to speak. "When is it?" he snapped.

"That's what we were trying to decide."

"I'm sure that now that Eden's hooked you she won't want to leave it too long, just in case you change your mind."

"I won't change my mind," Tim told him resentfully. "It's more likely to be the other way around."

"Oh, I doubt it," Jason drawled.

"Then you don't know her very well. Eden doesn't really want to get married for some time yet. She wants to travel first."

Jason gave her a hard look "Then why don't you?"

"I—"

"I don't want her to," Tim told him with youthful arrogance.

"Isn't that rather selfish of you? She's very young to

be tied down to a husband and possibly a young family.''

Tim flushed at the intended rebuke. "Why don't you—"

"Surely that's up to me to decide," Eden cut in smoothly, hoping to avoid an argument between the two men. They were like a couple of dogs scrapping over a favorite bone.

"Well?" Jason raised his eyebrows questioningly.

She glared at him. "I haven't decided yet."

He stood up. "You shouldn't leave it too long; rich young men like Tim don't grow on trees. Excuse me." He nodded distantly before leaving the room.

"Whew!" Tim muttered.

"It was your fault," Eden turned on him angrily. "You antagonized him."

"He didn't need much pushing."

"Maybe not, but you didn't have to tell him those lies."

"Why not? He was jealous as hell."

"Don't be ridiculous." She gave an impatient sigh. "You've just made it awkward for us to stay here now."

"I got the impression Jason wouldn't let us leave even if we wanted to—*you*, anyway. He'd probably throw me out if he could," he chuckled.

"Not when he's just invited you to stay."

"He's invited me to stay so that he can keep an eye on us. He's like a dog guarding a bone, a bone he's been saving for a special occasion."

Strange that he should use the same comparison as she had seconds earlier. "I wish you would stop saying things like that," she said irritably. "It simply isn't true."

"There's nothing simple about the way Jason feels about you. He eats you up with his eyes."

She put up a hand to her flushed face. "Stop it, Tim. You're embarrassing me."

"That's nothing to what Jason would like to do to you. I believe him when he says he isn't marrying Isobel Morton."

"It's what she says that counts at the moment. She's playing on the fact that she's in a distressed state to keep him constantly at her side. If he's not careful she'll trap him into marriage without his realizing it."

"If he lets that happen he's a fool."

She smiled. It sounded strange to hear a derogatory remark made about Jason; most people seemed to like him. "Come on, I'll show you to your room." It could only be one of two rooms, the others being occupied, and so she should have no trouble finding it.

"Is it next to yours?"

"No." She remembered Jason had said it wouldn't be, which was how she had narrowed it down to the two back bedrooms.

"By Jason's orders?" Once again Tim had guessed her train of thought.

"Yes," she reluctantly admitted.

"Is he sharing your room?"

She gasped. "Tim!"

"As I said, the man's a fool. I wouldn't pass up an opportunity like the one he's had."

"Tim, you know I don't—"

"Maybe you don't," he grinned. "But he does. And it isn't in him to deny himself something he wants."

"This is hardly the time," she reminded him. "We've had a family bereavement."

"Would you like me to come with you this afternoon?" he asked quietly.

"Do you want to? Funerals aren't very pleasant things."

He put his arm around her shoulders as they walked up the stairs. "I'm the nearest thing you have to family over here. As Jason will no doubt be with the lovely Isobel, I think it only fair that I should be with you."

"Thank you, Tim." She turned to kiss him.

"If you have to do that sort of thing perhaps you could find a more convenient place to do it than halfway up my stairs!"

Eden broke guiltily away from Tim's embrace, looking up to see Jason watching them from the top of the stairs. He had changed into a dark formal suit, his tie black. "Sorry," Eden mumbled, feeling about five years old as he watched the rest of their ascent with scornful eyes.

"I wouldn't have broken up that touching scene, but I happen to be in a hurry," he informed her coldly. "I'm lunching with Isobel before we go to the funeral," he explained.

"Oh," she nodded. "I didn't realize. Tim and I can get a taxi to the church."

"If it weren't for your ridiculous aversion to Isobel, you would be lunching with us. As it is, a car will pick you up at two-thirty. You and Tim, if he intends coming with you," he said impatiently.

"I do." Tim once again had his arm around her shoulders. "I think she may need me."

"I would have taken care of her if you hadn't arrived," Jason informed him haughtily.

"Well, now you won't need to bother," Tim told him in a dismissive voice. "If you'll excuse us, Eden is just going to show me to my room."

Jason gave her a cold look. "I wasn't aware that she knew which room had been prepared for you."

She bit her lip. "I...I don't," she admitted. "But it shouldn't be too difficult to find it."

"Maybe not, but I would prefer you not to play games in my bedrooms," he said harshly. "Or perhaps you were just going to take him to your own room and hope no one would notice?"

"Now look here—"

"It's all right, Tim," she soothed him, giving Jason a defiant look. "Maybe I was. It would have been so much better than having to sneak around the corridors in the early hours of the morning."

"Eden!" Tim gasped, a puzzled frown on his brow.

"Really, Tim, it's okay." She forced herself to smile. "We don't have to pretend in front of Jason. He knows very well that whether or not you have your own room you'll be sharing my bed."

"But, *Eden*—"

"I told you there's no need for pretense," she insisted.

"Too damned right there isn't!" Jason said savagely. "Just don't let me catch you," he warned darkly, "or you'll both leave here a lot quicker than you arrived. Tim has the room next to mine." He took the stairs two at a time and strode out, slamming the front door.

Tim frowned down at her. "What on earth was all that about? I realize Jason was jealous of my kissing you, and that he hit out because of that jealousy, but what I don't understand are the things you said to him. Why did you—"

"He expects it," she said with a sigh. "I was just making sure he wasn't disappointed."

"But surely he doesn't think we—"

"Oh, but he does," she laughed. "He's sure I'm trapping you into marriage."

"Arrogant devil!"

"He's more than arrogant, he's insulting. The only retaliation I have is to bait him."

"You sound as if you enjoy it."

"I do," she grinned. "If only to see him get good and mad." She looked at her wristwatch. "I'll show you to your room and then change for lunch. We don't want to be late for this afternoon."

THE FUNERAL was a curiously distant affair to Eden. Isobel Morton cried all the way through the service, leaning heavily on Jason, but Eden couldn't shed a single tear. She had cried herself out on Tuesday and now had nothing left to cry.

She was conscious of the curious looks of the other people at the funeral, but Tim proved to be very protective and didn't let anyone come near her. Fortunately, only the four of them returned to the Morton house. Isobel was now near to collapsing, although she refused to go to her room when it was suggested.

"I want to meet Eden's friend," she said shrilly, almost hysterically.

"I think you should go and lie down," Jason insisted softly. "You can meet Eden's friend some other time."

"But he may not be here another time." Isobel gave a malicious smile. "According to you, she changes her men with her nail polish."

"Isobel!" His mouth was a firm line of disapproval.

"Well, you did say that, darling." She gave them all an innocent look. "Or have I been indiscreet?"

Eden was very white. "You're upset," she said tautly. "I realize that."

"Upset or not, you must learn to guard your tongue, Isobel," Jason snapped. "We all realize how traumatic this has been for you—David's death, Eden's arrival—but there's no need to resort to insults."

"Jason!" Eden was aghast. What Isobel had said had been insulting, and it had hurt, but now was hardly the time to reprimand her. "It really doesn't matter."

"Yes, it does, damn you! I won't let—"

"I'm sorry, darling," Isobel said throatily, looking at him pleadingly.

"It isn't me you should be apologizing to." He was unyielding.

"Jason, please!" Eden protested once again. "Let's just forget it." Although the idea of his discussing her morals with Isobel Morton didn't appeal to her one little bit.

"Let's do that," Isobel agreed instantly, turning to look at Tim. "If no one else will introduce me I'll introduce myself. I'm Isobel Morton, and you must be Gary. Jason has mentioned you—"

"Gary?" Tim cut in suspiciously. "Who the hell is Gary?"

Isobel looked genuinely surprised. "You *aren't* Gary?"

"I'm Tim," he told her grimly. "And I thought I was Eden's boyfriend, possibly even her future husband. Who is Gary, Eden?"

She swallowed hard, knowing that her explanation wouldn't sound any better to him than it had to Jason—or be any more believable!

CHAPTER EIGHT

"WHO IS HE, EDEN?" Tim repeated the question some five minutes later.

Isobel Morton had taken that five minutes to escape from the situation she had just created. Jason had accompanied her, either through a desire to be alone with her or as a way of avoiding listening to Tim's questioning. Whatever his reason, he had left Tim and Eden alone.

"Gary, you mean?" she delayed.

"You know damn well who I mean," he snapped. "So?"

"He . . . he's just someone I met over here."

"Does Jason know him, too?"

"Er, no."

"Then how did you meet him?"

She sighed. "Jason would tell you that I let him pick me up. But it wasn't like that," she added hastily.

"Then how was it?" he asked coldly.

She could see his face darkening with anger as she explained how she had met and talked to Gary; the same anger and disgust that Jason had displayed.

"And why didn't you tell me about him?" Tim demanded.

"Because he wasn't important. And I—"

"He may not be important to you, but he's important to me," Tim interrupted fiercely. "And thinking about it, Jason could be right about the number of men you've had in your life. I seem to remember seeing you with at least half a dozen other men before we started dating, and none of them lasted very long.''

''That was because—''

''None of them had any money.'' He looked at her with dislike. ''I timed my proposal all wrong on Saturday, you said so yourself. You had just learned that you were going to get all your grandfather's money and so you didn't need a rich husband anymore. What you didn't know was that Jason would have control of the purse strings. I can see it all now, your eagerness for me to come to England when you realized you weren't going to be the little rich girl you had imagined you would be. Telling Jason you were going to marry me wasn't a defense at all. It was a trap—for me.'' He shook his head. ''And I nearly fell for it.''

Eden was very pale. ''Is that what you really think?'' she asked chokingly.

''What else is there?'' he said savagely. ''It's all been a game to you, hasn't it? I bet if Jason could be caught in the matrimonial trap he would be your number-one choice of a husband. After all, it would be so convenient, and as his wife I'm sure you could bring him around to your way of thinking about the money.''

''I'm sure I could,'' she retaliated, stung by his words. ''And what makes you think he isn't my number-one choice anyway? I could just be using people like you and Gary to bring him to heel. He wouldn't be an easy man to capture, and I would want marriage, not an affair.''

''You really would marry him if you had the chance?''

She shrugged. ''You said it, I didn't.''

''You calculating little—''

''Stop it, Tim,'' she said wearily. ''This isn't getting us anywhere. Either you believe me or you believe Jason. You have to make your own choice about that.''

''Well...there is this Gary. How did—''

"You obviously believe Jason. Now just for the record I'll tell you about the other men I dated before you. They didn't last for the simple reason that they weren't men, they were still boys, and they bored me. I thought you were different. I thought wrong."

His face took on a ruddy hue. "Are you saying I bore you?"

She had obviously hit him on the raw. "What's wrong, Tim? Does it hurt all that Channing pride that I don't just swoon at your feet? No, you don't bore me," she answered his question. "Your moods are too erratic for you to ever do that. Your Mr. Nice Guy image is at war with your Channing influence, and sadly, the latter is winning. You're still a little boy, Tim, a boy who has no idea what he wants except that it has to be the things he can't have."

"Meaning you?" he sneered.

She nodded. "Meaning me."

"According to Jason you're for sale to the highest bidder," he said nastily.

"You aren't the highest bidder," she told him in a bored voice, hiding her pain with an effort.

"I suppose Jason is that?"

"And if he is?" she challenged.

"Then I wish you luck," he taunted. "Because Jason is definitely a man who will never be faithful to any one woman. If you want that sort of life then that's just great, but if you don't...." He shrugged. "If you want him to be a one-woman man you're going to be disappointed."

"I have to completely eliminate the beautiful Isobel first."

"That should be quite easy; you have the advantage of sharing a house with him. It should be easy for you to sneak along to his bedroom whenever you want. And I intend removing myself as quickly as possibly, so you'll have a clear field in that direction."

"Oh, Tim," she sighed. "This isn't the way I planned your visit at all. I wanted—"

"I know what you wanted," he told her coldly. "You wanted Jason, this Gary and me, all on a bit of string until you decided which one to pull in. Well, I'm breaking loose. I'll let Jason and Gary fight it out between them."

"Since Gary doesn't have any money, I don't have much of a choice." She watched him stride toward the door. "Where are you going?"

"To collect my things," he said distantly. "I'll be gone by the time you return with Jason."

"But I came with you!"

"I'm going back to the States, Eden. Today."

"But—"

"Goodbye, Eden!" The room seemed to shake with the vibration as he slammed the door after him.

She hurriedly collected her handbag, intent on getting a taxi back to Jason's. How he would love it when he found out Tim had walked out on her!

She was just congratulating herself on her success when Jason spoke from behind her. "Don't you think it's bad manners just to leave?" he asked coldly, stopping her in the process of opening the front door.

Eden turned to face him, clutching her bag defensively in front of her. "I...I wasn't sure how long you would be," she offered lamely.

"You must have known I would be down soon. Today is hardly the time to even consider staying here."

"I wasn't to know that," she flashed.

"Try using your common sense." He came to stand beside her. "Isobel has taken one of the pills the doctor prescribed for her. She's fast asleep."

Eden bit her lip. "I see."

Jason looked around them pointedly. "Where's Tim?"

"He . . . he had to leave."

A mocking smile tilted his mouth. "Did he now?" he mused. "I take it he didn't like being mistaken for your friend Gary?"

"Would *you*?" she snapped.

He laughed. "I don't usually have those problems."

"I don't suppose you do—everyone knows the notorious Jason Earle."

"I'd advise you to guard your tongue," he told her tightly. "I'm not the best person to antagonize at the moment, not as far as you're concerned."

"What will you do—stop my allowance?" she challenged.

"I may just do that, so in future remember."

SHE HAD TO REMEMBER A LOT OF THINGS the next few weeks, the main one being to stay out of Jason's way. His mood and temper were unpredictable, her arguments with him numerous. She found it easier to stay out of his way wherever possible, although even that seemed to cause him to flare up angrily. Nothing she did seemed to be right, the main thing being his disapproval of her renewed acquaintance with Gary. The young painter had telephoned her as he had said he would, and they had met several times these past few weeks.

Gary was working in earnest in preparation for his exhibition, and Eden visited his combination flat-studio to see his paintings. Most of them she didn't understand, abstract art not being to her taste, but there were some landscapes and portraits that she rather liked. Gary was talented, of that she had no doubt. But he wouldn't be a success on his talent alone; he needed rich patronage, an influential client who would bring publicity to his work. He needed someone like Jason Earle.

"Jason...."

He scowled at her over the top of the papers he had spread before him on his desk in the study. "Yes?" he asked tersely, uninvitingly.

Eden entered the room anyway, used to his taciturn nature by now. "I've been thinking...."

"Oh, yes?" He sat back in his chair, watching her through narrowed eyes. "And just what have you been thinking?"

"Well...."

"Yes, Eden?" he prompted impatiently. "Hurry up, girl! I have work to do. Couldn't you have spoken to me about this over dinner?"

"You—you seemed preoccupied then." Oh, dear, perhaps this wasn't the time to discuss Gary's paintings with him.

"I'm preoccupied now." He indicated the papers on his desk. "Or can't you see that?"

"Anything I can help you with?"

His mouth tightened. "No."

She sighed. "Perhaps you're right; perhaps this isn't the time to talk to you."

"About what?" he snapped. "For God's sake, Eden, tell me what it is and then go. When I've finished this work I have to go and see Isobel," he said grimly.

"How is she?"

"Suicidal most of the time. Of course it could all be just an act, but I'm not willing to take the risk. Now what do you want to talk to me about?"

He did look tired, and if Isobel Morton was being difficult.... "Are you sure that work is nothing I can help you with?"

His harsh laughter rang out. "Are you by any chance trying to find out my private business?" he taunted.

"Certainly not! I just thought I might help—as a secretary. I wasn't trying to pry," she added resentfully.

"I forgot you're a qualified secretary," he said wearily. "Okay, I accept that you weren't trying to pry. But I don't need your help; I have a perfectly adequate secretary at my office."

"The girl who's never sick!" Eden remembered bitterly.

"That's right. Now what were these momentous thoughts of yours."

She flushed at his derision. "They aren't momentous."

"They aren't?" His eyebrows rose. "I felt sure they had to be, the way you forced yourself in here."

"I didn't force myself anywhere!"

"Like hell you didn't. Well, you can take yourself back out again if you don't soon say what you came to say. I think I've wasted enough time on you already."

"I'm sorry!" she snapped. "I'll go. I don't want you to *waste* any more of your valuable time on me."

He was out of his chair and standing in front of the door before she even reached it. "I can think of a way time spent with you would be far from wasted," he said huskily.

Her eyes were deeply golden. "Jason...."

"Mmm?" He moved to run one hand caressingly across her cheek and throat.

"Jason." Her tongue seemed stuck to the roof of her mouth. Jason hadn't attempted to touch her like this since before her grandfather's funeral, since the night he had presumed they would one day have an affair—since the night he had *decided* they would have an affair. "I wanted to discuss the house with you."

"The house?" He frowned, stepping back. "What house?"

"This house. I think—"

"*My* house?" He sounded astounded.

"Yes. You see—"

"What the hell does my house have to do with you? What say do you think you have in anything that goes on here?"

She recoiled. "I don't. I just—"

"You were just about to give me some helpful suggestions," he sneered. "Little helpful suggestions about the decor, I suppose?"

"Not—not actually about the decor."

His eyes narrowed. "About what, then? It's my house, Eden. You may be a guest here, but that doesn't give you the right to start reorganizing the household for me."

"I didn't think it did!" she said indignantly. "Stop twisting everything I say."

"You must admit that what you're saying does sound a little suspect. If you want to take an interest in any part of the house I would prefer it to be my bedroom."

"I wanted to discuss some paintings with you!" Eden snapped. "But if all you want to do is be insulting we can just forget about it." She turned to leave.

Jason swung her around. "What paintings?" he demanded suspiciously.

"Some of the rooms are a little bare. I just thought that you could buy one or two paintings to brighten the place up."

"What sort of paintings?"

"Oh, abstracts, landscapes," she said carelessly. "Anything to make the rooms more attractive."

"I've always thought they were attractive enough. They were designed by an expert."

"Maybe that's the trouble: they need a more homely touch. At the moment they look like something out of a furniture showroom."

"Why this sudden interest in how my home looks?"

She gave a casual shrug of her shoulders. "I was just trying to take an interest."

"Not considering moving in permanently, were you?"

"No, I wasn't! Don't worry, Jason, I'll be moving out soon. It was just that I saw some paintings the other day that would be ideal for the lounge."

"Where?" He sounded indulgent.

"Er, Gary has some—"

"Gary?" he echoed sharply. "What does Nichols have to do with this?"

Eden was surprised at his remembering Gary's surname. "He...he paints. And he—"

"My God!" He gave an astounded laugh. "You want me to buy paintings from your lover? Does he need paying for his services to you?"

"Jason!" She had gone very white.

"Jason, *what*?" he snapped. "Isn't your allowance enough to keep him in the fashion to which he's not accustomed?"

"You—you're disgusting! You can't mean what you're saying, Jason," she added pleadingly. "He's good, Jason, very good."

"Is he now?" he sneered. "I really don't want to hear about his sexual expertise."

She gasped. "That wasn't what I meant, and you know it! His paintings are very good, some of the best I've seen by an unknown artist."

"And what would you know about it?"

"Quite a lot, actually. Art is Drew's pet interest, and he's taught me to appreciate it, too."

"I still don't intend buying any paintings just to support your young lover. Forget him, Eden." His voice lowered seductively. "He can find his own way in the world if he's as good as you say he is. What I want to know is, when are you going to keep your promise to me?''

"Promise?" she delayed. "I don't remember promising you anything."

He laughed throatily. "Half promised, then. It's four weeks since the funeral, four weeks of patient waiting in which I haven't dared even touch you in case I lost control. But I intend to touch you now." He lowered his head, his lips caressing her throat. "More than touch you," he murmured.

Eden's pulse was racing, her senses spinning. "But, Jason, you said—you said you were going to see Isobel."

"She'll understand if I don't arrive."

She shivered as he gently bit her earlobe, strange fluttering sensations coursing through her body. "But you said she was suicidal. And she'll be expecting you."

"Not tonight," he told her with a shake of his head. "I didn't tell her I was coming; I just decided to go there because tonight I want you very much." His mouth was burning a trail of passion across her throat. "But now that I have you here I have no need to escape from thoughts of you with Nichols."

"But, Jason—''

"Just shut up, Eden," he ordered impatiently. "Shut up and kiss me. The time of waiting is over, and tonight I intend for us to share more than a house."

"Will it be your bedroom or mine?" she asked sarcastically.

"Mine." He didn't rise to her sarcasm, swinging her up in his arms and walking purposefully up the stairs. "I happen to have a double bed," he said, grinning down at her.

"How convenient!"

"Mmm." He kissed her briefly on the mouth, raising his head only to kick open the door to his bedroom.

Eden swayed slightly as he put her back on her feet. "Jason, we can't do this," she protested. *She* couldn't do it! "Jason, please stop," she pleaded as he lowered the zipper on the back of her gown. "Jason!" she gasped as he smoothed the gown from her shoulders and it fell around her ankles with a rustle of the soft material.

She blushed as he slowly appraised her almost naked body in the pink bikini briefs and matching pink bra, the lacy cups of the latter only just managing to maintain her modesty.

"Beautiful," he breathed softly. "But I knew you would be."

"You...you did?" She felt strangely mesmerized, held there against her will by the intimacy of his gaze.

"Mmm." He touched the firm swell of her breasts beneath their lacy covering. "Undress me, Eden."

"I...we.... The servants—" she stammered desperately, her hands covering her body as best she could.

"Are too discreet to interrupt. They certainly make themselves scarce when we're at home together."

"They don't think—" She swallowed hard. "Do they think we're having an affair?"

"Probably," he shrugged. "What does it matter?"

"It matters to me." She bent to pick up her gown. "Because it isn't true."

"Not yet." He took the gown out of her hands and threw it onto the bed. "Do you want to shower first or shall I?"

"Shower...?"

"Mmm. Better still, we'll shower together." He began unbuttoning his shirt with one hand, keeping a firm hold on her with the other.

Eden wrenched her gaze away from the seduction in his eyes, pulling out of his grasp to clutch her gown in front of her. "You just won't understand, will you?" she cried.

"I'm not promiscuous as you think I am. There's been no one in my life."

His eyes narrowed to icy gray slits. "What do you mean, no one?"

"I mean no *man*." She pulled her gown on over her head, pulling up the zipper with shaking fingers. "I've never been to bed with anyone, never given myself to a man."

"I don't believe you. Before you told me—"

"I told you exactly what you wanted to hear," she cut in angrily.

"You think I wanted to hear about your other men?" His anger exceeded her own. "My God, the very thought of them tortures me," he added with a groan.

"And yet you did want to hear that from me. You taunted me until I retaliated in the only way I could."

"In the only way you knew could hurt me," he corrected harshly.

"Hurt you?" she spat. "Nothing could hurt you. I could sleep with a hundred different men and you wouldn't give a damn as long as you could be one of them." Her voice had risen shrilly.

"Is that what you think?" His face was a livid mask of anger. "What you really think?"

"I know it!" She wrenched open the door.

"Where are you going?" Jason demanded.

"Out!" she snapped.

"At this time of night?"

"At any time of night, if I feel like going. Don't wait up for me—I'll be very late." She slammed the door after her, ran down the stairs to pick up her handbag and dashed out of the house as if the devil himself were after her. She needed her handbag because her car keys were in it, the keys to the car Jason had given her the money to buy, a bonus on top of the weekly allowance he gave her.

Her sports car was outside, and she got straight into it and drove off, anxious that Jason shouldn't even attempt to follow her. She didn't know where she was going, she just knew she couldn't stay in the house another minute with Jason.

She seemed to drive to Gary's flat without realizing it, the lights blazing in all of his rooms telling her that he was at home. It was ten-thirty, very late to be calling on someone, and yet she knew Gary kept strange hours. He probably wouldn't think anything of her turning up at this time of night.

She was right: he didn't. "Come in," he invited her, instantly throwing open the door. "Take a seat—I'm just in the middle of some work."

"Taking a seat" meant sitting on one of the cushions scattered around the floor, for Gary and his roommate, Sean, did not seem to believe in chairs. "I'm not disturbing you, am I?" she asked, watching as he carried on with his painting.

"Not at all," he answered vaguely.

"Where's Sean?"

"Staying at Annie's." Annie was Sean's girl friend of two years' standing. "How about making me some coffee?"

She stood up. "I hope you have some milk this time; I'm not partial to black coffee. You artistic types, you never think of practicalities like food and drink."

She made several cups of coffee for them during the next three hours, the last one black since, true to form, Gary didn't have enough milk. She watched him work, watched as his ideas went down on canvas, another abstract that she couldn't appreciate.

Finally he put his paintbrush down, rubbing his hands on an already paint-daubed cloth. He stood back, looking critically at his work. "Mmm, not bad," he said finally.

"I won't ask what it is," she teased. "I'm sure it's good, whatever it is."

Gary shook his head. "I'll have to teach you about abstract art. It's—"

"Not now, Gary," she laughed. "It's much too late in the day. I won't be able to take it in."

He looked at his wristwatch. "You should have stopped me from working—it must have been very boring for you."

"Not at all. I welcomed the peace it gave me." There hadn't been much of that lately!

He seemed to see her for the first time, taking in the full-length evening gown. "Were we supposed to be going out somewhere?"

She laughed. "No, I...I just left home in rather a hurry."

"Home?"

"Jason's house," she corrected blushingly.

"You're still staying there?"

"You know I am. But I'll be moving out now." As soon as possible! "It was only a temporary measure anyway." One she had been loath to break.

Gary frowned. "I don't want to get rid of you or anything, but aren't you here a little late?"

She bit her lip. "I was hoping you wouldn't notice." She knew that sometimes Gary didn't bother to go to bed at all.

"You're much too distracting for me to overlook you," he smiled. "Had a row with your guardian?"

She flushed. "He isn't my guardian; I have parents in the States. Jason just looks after the business side of my inheritance."

"While you rake in all the money."

She sighed. "Yes."

"So, have you argued with him?" He sat down on the cushion next to hers.

"Yes. I . . . I was wondering if I could stay here the night, especially now that I know Sean isn't here. I could have his room," she explained hastily, not wanting her intentions to be misconstrued.

His eyebrows rose. "You want to stay here?"

"I wouldn't be any trouble," she said eagerly. "You won't even know I'm here."

Gary laughed. "You have to be joking. A beautiful girl like you sleeping in my flat and I'm not supposed to know you're here!"

She gave him a nervous glance. "I just want somewhere to sleep for the night. There wouldn't be anything more to it."

He put his hand over hers. "I know that, Eden. We've become friends the past few weeks; I realize that's all we are. But it must have been some argument for you not to want to go back tonight."

"It was." She didn't enlarge on the subject. Somehow she didn't want Gary to know how close Jason had come to seducing her. She still blushed to think how he had taken her dress off and looked at her with undisguised desire.

"Then, of course you're welcome to stay. Just make yourself at home. Move in if you want to. Sean's at Annie's most of the time now, and you'll have to move out of Earle's house sometime."

"Thanks for the offer, but I don't think Jason would let me actually move in here."

"I'm not asking his permission and I wasn't aware that you needed it."

"I don't. But I don't see the point of antagonizing him needlessly."

Gary frowned. "Are you frightened of him?"

"Certainly not," she said indignantly—at least, not the way he meant. "But I couldn't move in here anyway; it wouldn't work." She smiled. "I like to sleep sometimes, and you don't seem to have any sense of night or day."

He laughed. "I suppose not," he yawned. "Although I'm tired now. You'll have to put fresh sheets on Sean's bed; he tends to forget."

"It won't take me long."

"Unless you would prefer to share my bed," he added mischievously.

"I don't think so." It was her second offer to share a man's bed in a matter of hours!

"I thought not. But it was worth a try. You go to bed; I might work a little while longer."

"But I thought you were tired?"

"I work better when I'm tired. You'll find the clean linen in Sean's wardrobe."

"Where else?" she teased.

"If you moved in you could take care of me."

"I admire your persistence, even if I can't say yes. Don't work too late."

She stripped the bed and put on the fresh linen, feeling so tired that she didn't even want to think. She could still hear Gary working as she fell asleep.

She was woken by a loud hammering noise, followed by raised voices. She blinked rapidly in an effort to collect her thoughts. It was almost four o'clock in the morning; who on earth could be calling this time of night? She knew Gary had some crazy friends, but—

The bedroom door flew open with a bang, and the light was callously flicked on. When Eden could focus she saw an enraged Jason standing in the bedroom doorway, a sleep-tousled Gary standing behind him. That Gary, too, had been woken from sleep was obvious from his hastily pulled-on denims and bare torso.

With frightened eyes Eden looked at Jason over the top

of the sheet. The angry glitter in his eyes and thinned taut-
ness of his mouth told her the extent of his anger: he was
just about at boiling point. "Jason ... " she said weakly.

"Yes—Jason," he snapped. "Get out of that bed, Eden.
You're coming home with me."

"How did you find me?" she quavered.

"I looked up your young friend in the phone book from
the vague account you once gave me of where he lived.
Now get out of his bed and come with me."

"Hey, you can't burst your way into my flat and issue
those type of orders," Gary protested bravely. "If Eden
wants to stay, then she stays."

Jason looked at him with glacial eyes. "One more word
out of you, Nichols, and I'll put you on the floor where you
belong," he told the younger man calmly.

Gary colored angrily. "Don't think you can intimi-
date—" He didn't get any further before a fist landed on his
jaw with a resounding crack, the force of the blow knocking
him to the ground.

"Gary!" Eden was instantly out of the bed, not caring
that she wore only the pink bra and briefs. She bent down
beside him as he lay dazedly rubbing his jaw. "Are you
okay?" she asked concernedly.

He gingerly tested his jaw. "I ... I think so. Yes, I'm fine.
And he did warn me." He grinned up at her ruefully.

She turned to glare at Jason as he still glowered down at
them. "You could have broken his jaw," she accused. "As
it is, he—"

"Will you get some clothes on," Jason ordered through
gritted teeth. "I realize we're both familiar with your
charms, but that's no reason for you to parade around half-
naked."

She blushed to the roots of her hair as she became conscious of her state of undress, hastily pulling a blanket from

the bed to cover herself. She couldn't look at either of them, her embarrassment too acute. But she hadn't thought of modesty when Jason had struck out; she'd been concerned only for Gary's welfare.

"I'll wait for you in the other room," Jason told her in a stilted voice. "I'll give you just long enough to put your dress on," he warned.

"I'd better go, too." Gary stumbled to the door. "Although I meant what I said, Eden—you can stay if you want to."

One look at the cold determination on Jason's face was enough to tell her she had little choice in the matter. "I think I'd better go," she said quietly. "But I'm sorry this *brute* hit you."

He rubbed his jaw. "He packs quite a punch."

"Nichols!" Jason snapped. "Get out of there so that Eden can get dressed."

Five minutes later Eden was seated next to him in his Jaguar, glancing nervously at his rigid profile. "You didn't have to hit him," she finally remarked.

"Under the circumstances I think I was quite restrained."

"Circumstances? What circumstances? Just because you have control of my money doesn't mean you have any say in what I do. I think it will be better if I just move out of your house. I'll look for somewhere else later today."

"You'll do nothing of the sort," he told her calmly. "You're staying right where I can keep an eye on you. And I'm warning you, if you ever run to another man after one of our arguments when we're married, I'll beat you, too."

Her mouth fell open. "Married?" she gulped. "You and me?"

"That's right. Just as soon as it can be arranged."

CHAPTER NINE

"Aren't you forgetting something?"

"Isobel," he said knowingly.

"She's only part of it," Eden snapped. "You're damned arrogant, assuming I would marry you even if you asked me."

"Wouldn't you?" He had parked the car in the driveway to the house, turning in his seat to look at her.

"No!"

"We'll continue this discussion inside." He dragged her into the house and into his study, closing the door firmly behind them. "Do you have any special reason for refusing me?" he asked tautly.

"Just a very obvious one," she said sarcastically. "We don't happen to be in love with each other."

"We don't?"

She gave him a sharp look, unnerved by the warmth in his gray eyes. "No," she told him uncertainly.

"I'm in love with you."

"You are?" she gasped.

He nodded. "Very much so."

Eden felt numb. "But you can't be!"

"But I am." He moved slowly toward her, his hands moving up to cup each side of her face as he gazed intently down into her eyes. "I love you very much. And I want you to be my wife."

"Is...is this some sort of joke?" she quavered. "If it is, it's in very poor taste."

"No joke, Eden. Or if it is," he added grimly, " I don't find it very funny."

Neither did she! "Don't you think you ought to make your position clear to Isobel before you talk to me like this?" she challenged.

He turned wearily away. "Do you think I haven't been trying to do just that?"

"You've been trying...?"

"Yes. I did take her out before you came back from the States with me, I admit I even thought about marrying her at one time, but it never got to more than a thought. I never told her I was going to marry her—not at any time did I do that. But since David died she's begun clinging to me, always wanting me around. I've tried to break away, but it's too soon, much too soon. I didn't intend telling you how I felt about you until I had the situation with Isobel firmly under control. I had hoped to hold things at bay until Isobel was strong enough to take the fact that any idea of marriage between the two of us was just a fantasy of her mind." His mouth tightened. "But you've forced the issue, you and your other men. I just can't stand back and watch this constant string of men passing through your life. And I could kill you for tonight!" He shook her hard, his fingers bruising her flesh where he held her. "How could you go to Nichols after the passion we had just shared?"

She felt as if her teeth were rattling in her head. "St-stop shaking m-me, Jason," she begged. "I can't think straight."

He stopped shaking her, but his fingers still bit into her flesh. "I want to do more than shake you," he told her furiously. "Finding you almost naked in Nichols's bed! God, I could beat you within an inch of your life!"

"I *was* *almost* naked, Jason," she said pleadingly. "Doesn't that tell you anything?"

His eyes narrowed to steely slits. "What do you mean?"

"If I had been to bed with Gary, if he had made love to me, wouldn't I have been completely naked?"

"Are you saying...?"

"I told you earlier tonight that I have never been to bed with a man. That's still true."

"Eden?" Uncertainty entered his voice for the first time.

Her eyes glowed. "It's true, Jason," she confirmed huskily.

"My God, the torture you've put me through!" He pulled her savagely against him, burying her face in the hair at his throat. "No other man? Really?" He still sounded unsure.

Her hands moved up over his shoulders to caress his nape, smoothing the thick hair that grew there. "Do you want proof?"

He drew back sharply, searching her features. "Proof?" he repeated softly.

Eden nodded. "Proof."

"But there's only one way— Eden, you love me, too!" His exclamation was triumphant.

"Yes!" Her smile was tearful.

His mouth claimed hers with a fierceness that took her breath away, grinding against hers for long dizzying minutes before gentleness took over. His lips teased and tempted until she increased the pressure in an effort to stop this torment of her senses.

Jason was shaking when he finally put her away from him, still maintaining a hold on her by his linked hands at the base of her spine. "When?" he demanded to know. "When did you fall in love with me?"

She gave a happy laugh. "I didn't suddenly say to myself, 'Hey, I love this man!'"

"I know that." He shook her gently. "But there must have been a time when you realized it."

"It was...it was the day after I arrived in England." Incredible that it had happened so quickly. Even more incredible that she should love a man she had started out hating.

He frowned. "That long ago?"

"Are you doubting me again?"

He shook his head. "Just thinking of all the time wasted. I think I've loved you since the first moment I saw you."

Eden laughed. "I can't believe that. You were hateful."

"Most men are when they get that trapped feeling, especially when they reach my age and think they have escaped the trauma of love."

"Trauma?" she repeated. "Is it really so bad?"

"No," he smiled. "It's just that we have the added complication of Isobel's possessive attitude toward me."

"God, yes!" She pulled out of his arms and turned away from him. "I'd forgotten about Isobel for the moment." She swung back to look at him. "Why did you get involved with her, Jason? Why even think of marrying someone you didn't love?"

He sighed. "Try to understand, darling. I'm thirty-six, the age when most men are married, with families. I've escorted many women the past fifteen or so years, and I thought I was past the age of finding there was such a thing as love, especially with a girl of twenty!"

"So you were going to accept second best," she said bitterly. "Enter into a marriage of suitability rather than wait to see if the real thing did exist."

He lifted her chin, his eyes coaxing as he looked down at her. "But I didn't. I swear to you that I have never discussed marriage with Isobel, that the idea of it is all on her side."

"But you admitted to thinking about it," she accused.

"Well, yes. But—"

"It's like a betrayal," Eden said chokingly. "You say you find it torture to think of me with other men. Well, I find it nauseous to think of you with her!" Her voice shook.

"I'm seeing her at the moment only because she seems to need me. It's you I love. One look at you and my orderly existence and cold-blooded plans for a loveless marriage went out of the window. I've kept you with me these past weeks against Isobel's pleadings; she would have been only too pleased to have you move in with her, probably because she could see what was happening between the two of us," he added derisively. "But I wouldn't hear of your moving out." His hands tightened. "I still won't. I want you here with me, Eden. I can't bear to let you out of my sight. I love you, and if you go away from me I think I'll die."

"Jason...." She gently smoothed his brow. "I never dreamed you could feel this way about me."

He planted a lingering kiss in the palm of her hand. "You still haven't actually told me you love me."

"I haven't?" Her eyes were wide.

"You know you haven't."

She smiled teasingly, standing on tiptoe to kiss him softly on the lips. "I love you," she breathed the words against his lips. "I really love you very much."

"Enough to stay here with me?"

"I can't, Jason. Surely you can see that knowing we love each other just makes it more difficult. I'll definitely have to move out now."

"I won't let you go, Eden," he said fiercely. "When the hell would I see you?"

"Whenever you wanted to. But I want no hole-in-the-corner affair with you. Until you're free of Isobel I don't want anything to do with you."

"I don't belong to Isobel—"

Eden wrenched out of his arms. "She thinks you do."

"Then I'll speak to her."

"When? Next month...next year? We have no way of knowing when she's going to be strong enough to stop relying on you."

"I won't let you go, Eden," he repeated firmly.

"I think maybe I should just go home until all this is sorted out."

"No!"

"Yes." She hated having to refuse his impassioned denial. "If Isobel should find out about us before you've had chance to tell her...." She shook her head. "That could be disastrous in her emotional state."

"You can talk of leaving me when you've just told me you love me?" He sounded agonized.

"You know what would happen if I stayed here," she said, blushing.

"Would that be such a bad thing? I want you so very much."

"I...I couldn't, Jason. I meant it when I said there has been no one, and there won't be until I'm married. I'm afraid I couldn't deny you if I stayed."

"Would it matter so much? The first time isn't very pleasant for a woman. It could ruin our wedding night."

She smiled. "Not that old trap, Jason," she mocked. "I've heard that if a man is experienced enough he can make even the first time wonderful. And no one could deny your experience." Bitterness had entered her voice over the last.

His hand caressed her nape. "I can't erase the past, darling," he said gently. "I can only assure you that the future belongs to you."

"I can't stay." She shook her head. "Not until you've told Isobel. What if she won't let go? What if she does something stupid? I couldn't live with that."

"Eden, please—"

The study door slowly opened behind them, and a rather frightened-looking Mrs. Gifford put her head around it. Relief flooded her face as she recognized her employer and his young guest. She smiled. "For a moment I thought we had burglars. It's after five o'clock in the morning, you know," she added worriedly. "Is there anything wrong?" She wrapped her quilted dressing gown around her ample frame.

"Nothing, Mrs. Gifford," Jason answered, at his most charming. "Miss Shaw and I were just talking together after being out for the evening, and forgot the time."

The housekeeper looked skeptical that any subject could be so interesting as to take them to this hour of the morning to discuss. "Well . . . if you're sure everything is all right?"

"Everything is fine," Jason answered her again. "You go back to bed. Miss Shaw and I were just going upstairs ourselves."

"Yes." Eden sprang into action, hurriedly moving past the housekeeper. "I'll go up now. Sorry I kept you, Jason." She didn't look at him again, almost running out of the door and up the stairs.

"Eden!" Jason had followed her and now stood at the bottom of the stairs. "Eden!" The desperation in his voice stopped her flight. She turned wordlessly toward him. "We haven't finished our . . . discussion," he told her huskily.

"I think we've talked enough for one night." She refused to respond to his unspoken plea. "I'll see you tomorrow."

With Mrs. Gifford still standing there he could do little to stop her. "Good night, Eden." His lips formed the words "my darling."

Eden ran to her bedroom, leaning back against the closed door, feeling as if she had been given happiness with one hand and had it taken away with the other. Jason's love was something she had wanted so desperately, and now that she knew she had it she wasn't sure she could accept it. Isobel Morton relied on him so heavily at the moment, might always rely on him; and no matter what the woman had once done to her and her family, Eden wouldn't be responsible for Isobel's harming herself in any way.

But Jason loved her! She hugged herself, twirling lightly around the room, her eyes ecstatic. This moment was hers, hers and Jason's; there would be plenty of time later to have her fragile happiness destroyed. Jason *loved* her! Arrogant, forbidding, often harsh Jason loved *her*. From their somewhat shaky start, the open hostility, love had somehow managed to blossom.

She fell asleep with a smile curving her lips, waking to find only four hours had passed since she had come to bed. It was a beautiful morning, the sun shining, the birds singing, making Eden want to be out in the clearness of this surprisingly warm day. She couldn't go back to sleep now anyway, so she might as well go out.

It was ten o'clock when she emerged into the sunshine, only to find that the sun had been deceptive: there was a definite frost in the air. Her brown cords and fitted brown shirt were complemented by the thick woolen thigh-length coat she wore, a handbag thrown carelessly over her shoulder.

She spent the morning very much as she had done that first morning in London, but feeling none of the loneliness and desolation she had felt then. It was almost lunchtime before she realized she hadn't even given Gary a thought. She suddenly knew she had to go and see him, to make sure he was all right.

It didn't take her long to reach his flat, although it took several knocks before she heard any sign of movement inside, and even then the footsteps sounded sluggish.

It was a bleary-eyed Gary who finally opened the door to her, the slight discoloration on his jaw evidence that there had been a lot of force behind Jason's blow.

"Come in," Gary invited, turning to walk back into the kitchen, where he appeared to have been in the process of making coffee. "Want some?" he queried.

Eden shook her head. "I just came to make sure you were okay. Jason was—he was very angry last night."

"I gathered," he said dryly. "But you're all right, aren't you?"

"Me?" she frowned. "I'm fine."

"I had a feeling you might be." He picked up his cup and walked through to the lounge, dropping down onto the cushions. "I gather he put that smile on your face?"

Eden blushed, the smile instantly fading. "Not in the way you mean."

He quirked an eyebrow. "And how do I mean?"

"You—you think we went to bed together when we left here."

Gary shook his head. "I know damn well you didn't."

"You do?"

"Of course," he grinned. "If you had slept together you would still be with him. He isn't the type to let you get up and leave him after only a couple of hours."

She blushed. "He could have gone out, too."

"Not his style; he isn't the 'love 'em and leave 'em' type. So, what did happen when you left here?" He looked interested.

"We...we talked."

"About what?"

"Oh, this and that."

"Mainly *that*, I'd say," he teased. "When does the Morton woman get the Big News?"

She moved uncomfortably. "I wish you wouldn't put it quite like that. It doesn't sound very nice."

"That's probably because it isn't. I'm happy for you, but as far as I can tell she gets a bit of a raw deal."

Eden frowned. "Aren't you rather jumping to conclusions about Jason and me?"

"Am I?"

"Well...."

"Of course I'm not," he grinned. "It was pretty obvious to me last night that the man's mad about you. I'm sure he's told you that by now, just happened to mention it in passing."

"Gary, please—"

"I take it you aren't moving out now," he continued. "No point really, not when you'll soon be back there as his wife."

"Gary—"

He gave her a sharp look. "He does have marriage in mind, I hope. Or is he planning just to have an affair with you?"

"Of course he isn't!" she said angrily. "I'm sorry he hit you, Gary, but that's really no reason for you to insult me. Jason is just caught up in a difficult position—"

"I wouldn't mind being caught between you and Isobel Morton," he chuckled.

"I'm sure you wouldn't."

He sighed. "I'm just annoyed because he's walked off with my girl."

She smiled. "I was never your girl."

"I was steering you in that direction. The man's a damned nuisance," he scowled. "Why doesn't he stick to just one woman?"

"I think he intends to."

"You?"

"Yes," she told him huskily.

He shrugged. "Then, that's that. Once a man like him declares ownership, the rest of us might just as well not exist. I take it you love him, too?"

"Yes."

"Shame." He shook his head. "When's the wedding?"

She looked away. "You're going too fast, Gary. I haven't said I'll marry him."

He whistled through his teeth. "I'll bet he doesn't like that."

"He doesn't," she admitted ruefully.

"Does he know you're here with me?"

She bit her lip. "No."

He raised his eyebrows. "I hope for your sake he doesn't find out."

Her head went back defiantly. "I'm not afraid of him. If he asks me I shall tell him." But there was no reason why he should ask, thank God!

"I wouldn't if I were you," he told her, rubbing his jaw. "I have firsthand knowledge of how fierce his anger can be."

"He wouldn't hit me!"

"That man is capable of anything if he's roused. Have you been out of the house long?"

She shrugged. "A few hours, I suppose."

"Then, if I were you I would get back home, otherwise he's likely to come looking for you. And I don't think I'm up to another punch-up."

"He won't come looking for me," she laughed. "He's at work."

"Sure?" He sounded doubtful.

"Jason never takes time off unless he absolutely needs to." As on the occasion of her grandfather's funeral.

"Not even to be with the girl he loves?"

Eden laughed. "Can you see Jason as the sentimental type?"

"Quite frankly, no."

"Neither can I, so stop worrying."

She stayed with Gary for more than an hour, preparing a snack lunch for them both before she left. They parted friends, although Eden had no idea when she would see him again. She still hadn't made up her mind whether to go back to the States or simply find herself an apartment or flat in London. The latter was very tempting; she would still be able to see Jason that way.

She let herself into the house and was halfway up the stairs when she heard a firm familiar tread behind her. She spun around. "Jason!" Her eyes lighted up with pleasure and she ran down the stairs toward him, only to come to an abrupt halt two feet away from him, the anger in his face telling her of his displeasure. "Jason?" she frowned.

"Where have you been?" There was barely controlled violence in his voice.

"Jason?"

"Have you seen Nichols this morning?" His mood was dangerous.

"I—"

"Have you?" he demanded, the violence beginning to be unleashed.

"Jason, let me—"

"Have you?"

"Yes!" she answered as forcefully.

"You little bitch!" He swung away from her and slammed into his study.

Eden stood in dazed silence for several long minutes, and then she was galvanized into action, moving hurriedly to his study. He hadn't been to work; the faded denims and casual shirt he wore were evidence of that. He must have been waiting for her return all morning. And she had had to admit to seeing Gary. God, what must he think of her!

She received no answer to her tentative knock on the door, finally letting herself in. Jason was slumped behind the desk, his face buried in his hands. She couldn't bear to see him like this, and she moved to the back of his chair to pull his head back against her breasts. She caressed his temples to soothe him.

"Oh, God, Eden—" he turned his face against her "—don't torture me anymore. I can't stand it."

"I don't mean to, Jason." Her softened gaze rested on his bent head. "I went to see Gary only to—"

"I don't want to know!" he said fiercely, swinging the leather chair around to look at her. "Whatever there is between you two, I don't want to know about it."

"Let me finish, darling." She pushed the dark hair back from his furrowed brow. "I just wanted to make sure he was all right after you hit him." Teasing entered her voice.

"It didn't take you four hours to find that out," he scowled.

"No," she agreed. "I felt so good, so happy, that I went for a walk before going to see him."

"If you felt that good, why didn't you walk down the corridor to my bedroom? I would have welcomed you with open arms."

She smiled. "I thought you had gone to work."

"I stayed at home with the intention of spending the day with you." He grimaced. "I wasn't pleased when I found your bedroom to be empty."

"What would you have done if it hadn't been?" she asked softly.

"This," he groaned, pulling her head down so that their lips met in a searing kiss. "And this—" He kissed her throat, slowly unbuttoning her blouse, his lips moving down to the hollow between her breasts. "And this—" He released the front fastening of her bra to plunder the rosy peaks below. "Oh, God, yes, *this*."

Eden had known herself lost at the first touch of his lips on hers, and now she held him to her by her fingers entwined in the dark thickness of his hair. He pulled her down so that she lay across his lap, his lips on hers while his fingers caressed her, transporting her into a world of heady delight.

"I love you," she murmured throatily.

"And I love you," he moaned, his desire unhidden as he kissed and caressed her to meet his passion.

"If you believe that, then you're a fool," drawled a feminine voice from behind them.

"Isobel!" Jason stood up, pushing Eden behind him as she endeavored to tidy her clothing. "Isobel ..." he repeated.

"Yes!" Brown eyes flashed as she slammed the door behind her. "I should have known what was going on, I suppose," she sneered. "I must congratulate you on succeeding so quickly, Jason."

Eden was rapidly buttoning her blouse, her fingers seeming to be all thumbs in her haste. God, it was bad enough that anyone should find Jason and her in such an embarrassing situation, but that it should be Isobel Morton...!

"What is that remark supposed to mean?" Jason appeared completely calm.

Isobel smiled, a smile that held no humor. "I've been expecting this ever since you brought her back here."

Eden moved from behind Jason, a deep color in her cheeks. "I—it was just one of those things. There was nothing more to it than heightened emotions," she lied.

"Eden!" Jason gave her a furious look. "Don't make matters worse."

"Is that possible?" Isobel asked in a bored voice, looking coolly beautiful in a silky cream-colored dress that showed the slender curves of her body to perfection. "Really, Eden, you don't have to lie to me. I've known Jason a lot longer than you have, and I know exactly the way his devious mind works. Besides, I heard your declarations of love, remember?"

"Just the heat of the moment," Eden protested, although she had to admit this woman didn't look unduly concerned about finding her in Jason's arms. Perhaps it was going to be all right after all.

"I'm sure," Isobel agreed. "Jason is very good at making one forget everything but him, very accomplished."

"Yes ..." she said miserably.

"No need to look so upset, Eden," Isobel taunted. "I told you, I know Jason—very well, in fact." She turned to look at him. "When did you intend telling me of your forthcoming marriage? I take it there is to be a marriage?"

"Yes," he said grimly.

"That's what I thought. It would have to be marriage, wouldn't it, otherwise there would be no point to this. It's really too bad I had to upset David as I did. If he hadn't died I would probably have been Mrs. Jason Earle by now."

"*You* upset him." Jason demanded to know.

"Not intentionally, I can assure you. As I just told you, his early death was not part of my plans," Isobel said calmly. "In fact, just knowing I was partly responsible has made me feel ill these past few weeks. Buy I really couldn't let his new will stand unargued by me. I'm sure his will must have come as something of a surprise to you, too, darling."

"I knew about it before he died," Jason informed her tautly.

"But not all of it, and not long before, either. Am I right?"

He shrugged. "You could be."

"Poor Jason. What a shock for you," she laughed.

"Not at all," he dismissed the suggestion. "It was only to be expected that David would leave everything to his grandchild."

"A grandchild you didn't even know existed. It altered your plans somewhat, didn't it?"

The conversation was mainly passing over Eden's head, although she had registered the fact that Isobel was taking the blame for David Morton's second and fatal heart attack. Her own feelings of guilt faded. Isobel hadn't seemed at all upset or surprised at finding her and Jason in a passionate clinch, and although Eden could only feel grateful that they hadn't been subjected to a scene, it was a surprising reaction, almost as if Isobel had been waiting for this to happen.

"I had no plans, Isobel," Jason said calmly. "I knew that I was to be responsible for David's business affairs after his death, but I could have no idea—" he reached out to entwine his fingers with Eden's, smiling down at her "—that I was going to fall in love with his granddaughter."

"Oh, spare me that," Isobel snorted. "You may be able to dupe this lovesick child with that rubbish, but you and I know the truth. And this has nothing to do with your loving her. But I congratulate you on managing to make her fall in love with you."

"Shall I leave the two of you alone to talk?" Eden looked pleadingly at Jason, but he refused to let go of her hand, keeping her at his side.

"Certainly not," Isobel laughed. "This concerns you as much as it concerns us—more so, in a lot of ways."

"I...I'm just sorry you had to find out like this," Eden said awkwardly.

Isobel looked bored. "I didn't find out 'like this,'" she said. "I knew as soon as David told me he had left you in Jason's control that this would happen. Jason is too much the businessman to let this slip out of his grasp. But you'll be the only one to get hurt, Eden, I can assure you of that. Men like Jason never get hurt; you can't if you have no heart, and ice in your veins."

Eden frowned at yet another person's likening Jason to ice. "I don't understand what you mean. Let *what* slip out of his grasp?"

Isobel gave Jason a searching glance. "She still doesn't know?"

He looked at her coldly. "Isn't that obvious?"

"None of it?"

"No," he confirmed harshly.

"I suppose you were saving that for *after* the wedding."
She laughed. "My God, you really are a devious swine."

"What don't I know?" Eden demanded, tired of being
ignored. "Jason? Tell me!"

He looked at her with remote eyes. "Isobel can tell you.
I'm sure she'll enjoy it."

"I certainly will," Isobel confirmed.

"Then tell me," Eden said impatiently. "But just stop
talking around me. I want to know what's going on."

Isobel sat down, crossing one silky leg over the other. "I
think maybe you should sit down, too," she suggested.
"I'm going to knock your romantic daydreams about Jason
right out of the sky."

"I'll stand," she refused stiffly.

"Please yourself," Isobel shrugged. "Then I'll begin,"
she said maliciously. "You obviously know that Jason is
your financial guardian, but do you know why?"

She looked puzzled. "Because my grandfather trusted
him."

Isobel smiled. "Oh, yes, he did that. He trusted him because he was his *partner*."

"P-partner?" Eden looked at Jason with startled eyes.

Isobel nodded. "It wasn't a well-known fact, and in latter
years David had kept it pretty much to a financial partnership. That suited Jason; he always preferred to work alone
anyway. He would have bought David out if he could, but
David always refused." Her mouth tightened. "That was
when Jason decided that if he couldn't buy him out he
would have it when he died, by marrying me."

"Yes?" Eden prompted, feeling sick. And she had a feeling there was worse to come.

"Then David dropped his bombshell: he wasn't leaving it
all to me at all; he was leaving it all to his granddaughter.
Even then I don't think Jason was too perturbed, believing

he could persuade your mother to sell out to him. And then he met you. You were a great shock to him, Eden, not a child at all. You're twenty years of age, capable of making your own decisions, and with a strong mind of your own, too."

Jason remained silent through all this, curiously remote as he gazed out of the window, his attention apparently on the view in front of him. Eden wished he would say something, anything, but his profile remained rigidly turned away from her. If he would just once look at her with love in his eyes she'd be reassured, but he either was ignoring her silent pleadings or was unaware of them.

"I haven't finished yet." Isobel drew Eden's attention back to herself. "You see, there was a clause in David's will that even Jason didn't know about until after his death."

"Yes?" Eden asked dully.

"Even if you wanted to sell and Jason wanted to buy, which he obviously wishes he could, you aren't allowed to sell out to him or anyone else. The partnership has to stand."

"Then he has nothing to worry about, does he?" Eden snapped, Isobel's implication now explicit. And still Jason didn't defend himself!

"He would if you married," Isobel announced triumphantly.

Eden looked startled. "If I married...?"

"Mmm," the other woman smiled. "When you marry, your husband takes control, and Jason gives up any say in your side of the partnership. So now you know why Jason has to marry you. He simply doesn't want anyone else involved in his empire."

Eden was white, deathly white, her eyes glazed with pain as she turned to look at the man still staring rigidly out of the window. "Jason?" she choked. "Jason, is this true?"

CHAPTER TEN

IT WAS GOOD TO BE HOME, good to be back among the people who loved her, people who weren't trying to deceive her. Fortunately, Drew hadn't given her job to someone else, just employing temporary help until her return; and in the past year she had slotted herself back into her job and life as if she had never met and fallen in love with Jason Earle.

But her aching heart knew she had met him, the heart that had shattered into tiny fragments at Jason's refusal to defend himself. His silence had confirmed his guilt, and she had left England the next day, her heart broken, but a new determination about her that warned men off her by the dozen

She hardly ventured out of her home anymore; preferred staying in her bedroom listening to records or quietly reading to accepting any of the invitations she received.

If Jason had scorned her meriting her job as a secretary with Drew's firm, then he would now have to change his opinion. She had become the perfect secretary, always punctual, her work accurate and fast, with no complaints from her if she was asked to work late. Maybe Jason's opinion of her as a spoiled little brat had once been true, but it certainly wasn't now.

She hadn't heard from Jason or tried to contact him herself since her hurried departure, and as far as she knew he could now be going out with Isobel Morton again. She knew nothing about him, wasn't interested in knowing; any correspondence concerning her inheritance passed between Drew and Jason, at her request. Things appeared to be going well in that direction; the monthly checks she received were enough to keep her in luxury should she choose to live that way.

Her mother had changed on Eden's return, her appreciation of Drew as a husband dulling the sharpness of her tongue. As Drew had predicted, he had become his wife's strength, and to Eden they looked happier than ever.

She hurried home to dinner, her mother's telephone call earlier having urged her to do so. Something must have happened to make Angela so agitated, but she had refused to say what it was over the phone.

"Isobel Dean came here today," her mother burst out as soon as Eden came through the front door.

"Isobel Morton, mother," Eden said stiffly. "What did *she* want here?"

"Even that isn't her name now," her mother said disgustedly. "She's married again."

Eden paled drastically. "M-married?"

"Mmm. She came here just to flash her diamond engagement ring at me, I'm sure she did."

Jason had married the other woman after all! "Why did she say she came?"

"To see you, she said." Angela rearranged some roses in a vase standing on the coffee table. "I think she came just to crow over her good fortune in trapping a millionaire."

How could he! If she had ever doubted her mistrust of Jason, it had now been confirmed in a way that was irrefutable. He must have loved Isobel all the time; and when it became obvious that his plans had gone wrong, he had married the other woman after all.

"I—is she coming back?" God, not with Jason, please! That she couldn't bear.

Her mother shook her head. "She said she doesn't have time, that this was just a lightning visit, part of her honeymoon."

"H-honeymoon?" Eden echoed dully.

"Mmm," Angela grimaced. "She and her husband have been traveling the world as their honeymoon. She's just as much of a bitch as she always was. She came here only to show us that David's will meant nothing to her."

Apparently not, if she had married Jason after all. "I think I'll have dinner in my room." Eden's eyes were shadowed.

"Oh, you can't do that," her mother told her. "You're going out to dinner."

Eden sighed. "Where to this time?" Her parents had been arranging these invitations to dinner parties the past few weeks, deciding she didn't go out enough. But after what she had just been told she didn't think she could bear to sit down to dinner with other people and make polite conversation.

"*We* aren't going anywhere, but you are. Tim telephoned this afternoon and invited you out. I accepted for you."

"Tim Channing?"

"But of course, darling. I didn't think you knew any other Tim."

She didn't, and she didn't want to know this one anymore, either. "You had no right to accept on my behalf," she said tautly.

"It's high time you mended this silly rift between the two of you. He's done nothing but call you the past six months. And you look like a ghost walking around the house."

"But not because of him, mother," Eden cried impatiently.

"Of course it's because of him," Angela dismissed her

daughter's protest. "You weren't over there long enough to meet anyone else of importance. Besides, you admitted that you argued with him while you were there."

"Yes, but—"

"Stop being silly, Eden," her mother snapped. "Tim is a very nice young man, and—"

"He wasn't very pleasant to me in England."

"I'm sure you must have done something to anger him."

Oh, yes, she had angered him, but he had jumped to conclusions. "I don't want to go out with him." .

Her mother shrugged. "He's going to be here at eight-thirty. Drew and I are going to the Merricks', so you'll have to tell him yourself."

"I'll ring him," Eden said adamantly.

"I give up!" Her mother stormed off.

Eden wandered into her bedroom, closing the door behind her, automatically switching on one of the slow records that were always on the turntable nowadays. She didn't hesitate to call Tim, determined not even to see him, but was met by the constant ringing of the phone bell. She tried again, in case she had dialed a wrong number, but there was still no answer.

At eight-fifteen she had still received no answer to her frequent calls, giving up as she realized he would be on his way by now. She could always send him away when he got there.

And yet she found herself getting ready for her date with him, choosing to wear a black gown that gave her an air of sophistication, a cool hauteur that was impregnable. Right on time she heard the doorbell ring, and sounds of the maid showing Tim into the lounge.

He hadn't changed at all, still had the same boyish good looks, shown to advantage now in a black dinner suit and snowy white shirt. His eyes darkened appreciatively at her cool beauty. "Hi," he said huskily, obviously unsure of his welcome.

"Hello," she returned coolly. "Drink?" She indicated the tray of bottles on the table.

"No, thanks." He put his hands nervously into his trouser pockets. "I...I've booked a table at Delanie's. Is that all right with you?"

Delanie's! Oh, God, that was where she had first danced with Jason!

"We can go somewhere else if you would prefer it," Tim interpreted her expression correctly. "Just name the place and we'll go there."

She shook her head. "I—" she bit her lip "—I don't—"

His shoulders slumped. "You don't want to go anywhere with me, do you? I knew it when the telephone kept ringing again and again. It was you, wasn't it, calling to cancel tonight?"

Her eyes were wide and very golden. "You were there all the time?"

He nodded. "Afraid so."

"Then why on earth didn't you answer?" she demanded crossly, thinking of all the time she had wasted.

He gave a deep sigh. "Because I didn't want you to cancel."

"I can't think why. I thought we said all we had to say to each other over a year ago."

"I said altogether too much. I couldn't have been thinking straight or I would never have believed what I did. You just aren't capable of the things I accused you of. Jason told me I was an idiot, and—"

"When did he tell you that?" she interrupted sharply.

"Yesterday. But I knew before that. These past six months—"

"You saw Jason yesterday?" she cut in again.

"Mmm, he's in the States."

Of course he was! If Isobel was here it naturally followed that Jason was here, too. "I didn't realize you were such good friends that he would make a social call on you," she said sarcastically.

Tim laughed. "We aren't friends at all, you should know that. I saw him and Claire at the—"

"Jason and *Claire*?" she asked disgustedly. "Jason was out with your sister last night?"

"I told you before, whenever Jason is in town Claire goes running."

"Yes, but—" My God, even on his honeymoon Jason couldn't stay away from other women! She forced a bright smile to her lips "Delanie's, I think you said?"

His expression brightened. "You mean you'll come?"

She laughed. "But of course. Let's go."

It was a gay evening, an evening of laughing and talking, and dancing until her feet ached. It was as if she were trying to exorcise Jason from her mind and body for good, trying to erase him even from her thoughts.

And to a certain extent she did it, Tim setting out to be his most charming and so making it easy for her. The warmth of the alcohol she consumed put a sparkle in her eyes and heightened the color in her cheeks.

She collapsed against Tim after a more than usually exuberant dance. "Shall we sit down now?"

"Certainly not," he grinned. "They're playing our tune."

"*Our* tune?" She raised her eyebrows.

"Well, it could become our tune. It's nice and slow, and I'll get to hold you in my arms."

Eden smiled. "I'm not sure I should encourage you."

He pulled her close against him. "Oh, encourage me, Eden. Encourage me," he urged.

She laughingly moved away, all humor dying from her

face as she recognized the couple dancing beside them. Jason and Claire! And from the contemptuous look in Jason's glacial eyes, he had been watching her for some time.

Tim spotted the other couple more or less the same time she did, groaning against her ear. "Oh, God, why did they have to be here! I need them like I need a hole in the head," he muttered forcibly.

After that single meeting of their eyes Eden had turned hurriedly away from Jason, the beautiful kittenish Claire snuggled into his arms. "Could we leave?" she asked Tim in a strangulated voice.

"Not without looking rude. Look, we'll just say a quick hello and then get out of here. Okay?"

"Okay," she nodded, standing mutely at his side as he spoke amiably to the other couple.

"Dance with me!" Jason dragged her away from Tim and Claire, pulling her ruthlessly into his arms.

"Jason!" She raised a startled face. "Wasn't that rather rude?"

"Rude, hell!" he groaned, the roughness of his chin gently scratching her temple as he held her to him. "How have you been?" he asked huskily.

Couldn't he see? Couldn't he see by the gauntness of her face and the dark hollows beneath her eyes that she was dreadfully unhappy? "I'm very well, thank you. And you?"

"I'm well, too."

He didn't look it, either. On closer inspection he didn't look well at all. She had thought him haughty and withdrawn the first time she had ever seen him, but now his face was a cold hard mask, completely emotionless as he looked down at her. And he was thinner, too, the lines of dissipation deeply etched into his skin, his hair much too long and growing out of style. Only five percent of the iceberg was visible now, the freeze almost complete.

"I'm glad," she returned coolly.

"Are you?" he asked bitterly. "I doubt it."

"Probably not," she accepted without demur.

His mouth twisted. "Definitely not."

"What did you expect?" Her voice was calm, but her eyes flashed anger. "That I would be pining away for you?" And hadn't she been? Hadn't she!

He smiled without humor, his expression unpleasant. "Hardly," he mocked. "How long have things been back on with Tim?" he demanded harshly.

"Back on?" she frowned.

His hands at her waist were painful. "Yes, *back on*," he said grimly.

"Oh, I see what you mean." She gave a taunting laugh. "Quite some time," she lied. "You can expect to hear the sound of wedding bells in the near future."

"You're going to marry him?" he asked in a strangled voice.

"How will you like that, Jason—Tim as your partner?"

"I couldn't give a damn about the partnership!"

"I'll bet," she taunted. "Tim may be young, but he has a business mind. He'll have ideas he will want put into action."

"I'm still the senior partner; I always have been. Come on." He held her wrist in a viselike grip and dragged her back to where Tim and Claire were talking together. "Let me know when the wedding is," he said, his mouth twisted. "I'll try to make it."

"With Isobel?" she taunted.

Jason stiffened. "I can't speak for her. We live our own lives."

"I'm sure that suits you."

"It does," he agreed coldly.

"I'll let you know about the wedding." She turned and

put her hand through the crook of Tim's arm. "Ready, darling?" she smiled at him.

Tim blushed at the unexpected endearment, taking full advantage of her sudden change of attitude to put his arm possessively around her shoulders. He shrugged at the other two. "Excuse us. No man could refuse the invitation of being alone with Eden—could he, Jason?" he added with malicious enjoyment.

Jason's cold gaze was insulting as it swept over her. "Few do," he drawled.

Eden colored angrily. "Few get the chance," she snapped. "Tim?"

He shrugged. "Okay, let's go."

When they reached her home, Tim parked and turned in his seat to look at her. "You're very quiet," he observed caressing her pale cheek.

"Sorry." She gave him a strained smile. "I think I'm getting my hangover early." She certainly deserved one, considering the amount of alcohol she had consumed in the past few hours.

"It's Jason, isn't it?" He wasn't deceived.

"No!"

"Yes," he said firmly. "You still love him."

"I hate him," she cried, her voice breaking. "I hate him, I tell you!" Tears were streaming down her cheeks by this time, tears that she had held within her for the past year.

Tim gathered her to him, cradling her in his arms. "You love him," he stated dully. "I wish you didn't, but you do."

"I don't," she sniffed. "How could I love someone like him, someone who has no morals, someone who's with another woman even on his honeymoon!"

"Honeymoon?" He held her away from him. "Jason isn't on his honeymoon," he said scathingly.

"He is," she insisted, still crying, seeming unable to stop. "He married Isobel Morton."

Tim shook his head. "I don't know where you got your information from, but it's wrong. Jason isn't married to Isobel Morton or anyone else: he isn't even particularly interested in women at the moment."

"I suppose that's why he's with Claire," she said dryly.

"He's with Claire because my big sister doesn't know when to take no for an answer. And you can believe that Jason has been saying no. He isn't married, Eden," he told her again.

"But he has to be! Isobel came to see me this afternoon. She spoke to my mother—she said she was on her honeymoon."

"I'll bet your mother enjoyed seeing her again after all these years," he said speculatively.

"I don't think it particularly bothered her." With the death of David Morton, her mother finally seemed to have given up the past. Isobel's visit that afternoon didn't appear to have bothered her unduly.

"Did Isobel specifically say Jason was her husband?"

"I just assumed...." Eden frowned. Isobel Morton had known exactly what she would think; it had been her final gesture of hatred. "Oh, God," she groaned. "And I told Jason I was going to marry you." She was very pale.

"And again you didn't mean it," he sighed.

"I'm sorry. I didn't mean to use you, but Jason was being so insulting and—"

"Of course he was being insulting." Tim spoke to her as if she were a particularly stupid child. "The poor guy's mad about you, insane with jealousy if I so much as look at you."

"No...."

"Oh, yes," he insisted. "I don't know why the two of you split up, but that you love each other is plain to see. Even my particularly dense sister could see it. You should have heard her bitching about you when you were dancing with him."

"When he *forced* me to dance with him!"

"He just wanted to get his arms around you. He was like a thirsty man in a desert."

"Icebergs can't survive in a desert," she told him absently. Could it be true that Jason still loved her? If he did, she would go to him no matter what his reasons were for wanting her. She just couldn't live without him anymore.

Tim frowned. "Icebergs? What do icebergs have to do with this conversation?"

She smiled. "You wouldn't understand."

"Remembering another conversation we had about icebergs, I think I do," he said slowly. "And as far as Jason is concerned, you have the wrong comparison. He goes up in flames whenever you're around."

She blushed. "Do you really think he loves me?"

"I don't really think you need me to tell you that." He restarted the car engine. "I'll take you to his hotel."

"I—he won't be there yet."

"Then you can wait for him."

"What if Claire—"

"I told you, he's not interested in her."

"What if the same applies to me?" she asked worriedly.

He gave her an impatient glance. "Where were you when feminine intuition was being handed out?" He shook his head. "Jason loves you. It's up to you to get him to admit it."

Remembering the things she had believed about him, things she now knew he couldn't possibly have done, she didn't think that was going to be easy.

Tim saw her frown. "I'm sure you'll think of a way to persuade him round," he teased.

She blushed. "You're being very kind to me."

"I'd rather it was me you loved, but if I can't have you I'd like to see you marry someone who's going to make you happy. And Jason seems to be the man you want. I hope you get him."

The hotel lobby was strangely quiet and deserted this time of night, only the night porter behind the desk to eye her occasionally as she sat waiting. She was very nervous, constantly looking at the huge double-glass doors, longing for and yet dreading Jason's arrival. After all, she had only Tim's opinion that Jason loved her.

Her heart leaped as she saw him enter the hotel, completely alone, his expression remote as he nodded to the night porter. He came to a sudden halt as she stepped out from behind the huge potted plant that had shielded her from curious eyes, taking an involuntary step toward her and then stopping, a fierce flame burning in his eyes, a flame that told her all she needed to know. Jason did love her!

"Eden?" His voice was husky, demanding.

She swallowed hard. "Jason—" her tongue seemed to be stuck to the roof of her mouth "—I...I love you," she told him chokingly.

He took hold of her arm, his remoteness becoming a thing of the past. "Let's go up to my suite."

"I thought you didn't like young girls calling on you here," she said stupidly, remembering their first conversation.

He raised dark eyebrows. "Are you calling on me? I thought you had come to stay," he said throatily.

Love blazed in her eyes. "Jason...."

"Wait until we get upstairs, darling." He held her tightly

against his side. "If I start kissing you here I'm never going to stop."

As soon as they entered his suite he turned to pull her into his arms, easing her lips apart with the tip of his tongue, tasting the sweetness within like a man deprived of his life's force. His hard body was pressed against her, making her aware of his desire.

She clung to him, meeting the demand of his kiss with equal fervor, her arms thrown around his neck as she arched her body against him. If he chose to make her his right now she wouldn't object, the past year without him having shown her that all she wanted was him.

"God, I needed that." He drew a ragged breath, taking hold of her hand and leading her over to the sofa, lying down beside her on its length. "I'm not letting you out of my sight again tonight," he groaned.

She moved to slip his jacket from his shoulders, slowly unbuttoning the silk shirt to run her fingertips caressingly over his taut skin. "I love you, Jason." She was unashamedly offering herself to him. "I belong to you."

He closed his eyes, opening them again to stare at her as if he couldn't believe she was really there. "God, I've missed you, Eden." He caressed her throat with hard kisses. "This is what you want, isn't it?" he gasped. "It's what you were saying downstairs just now?"

"Oh, yes, yes!" She felt light-headed.

"You are mine, aren't you?" he demanded. "You don't belong to Tim?"

"I lied, Jason, I lied."

"Hurting me again." He sounded agonized.

"I'm sorry." She rained fevered kisses over his face. "I've just been so confused." She told him of Isobel's visit and of how she had thought he was the other woman's husband.

"I wouldn't marry her under any circumstances," he said fiercely. "But no doubt you're right in her wanting you to think that. Isobel is still a very bitter woman. I have no idea why; she seems to have everything she could ever want. She's married to a Greek millionaire whom she met on the cruise she took just after you left England."

She felt him shudder as he remembered her hurried departure. "I should never have listened to her. I should have trusted you, shouldn't I, Jason?"

"The basic outline of what she said was true; it was only the emotions she missed out. You couldn't possibly have trusted me—you didn't know me well enough. Trust comes with knowing a person for a long time."

She pressed herself against him. "This sort of knowing?"

"No." He gave a husky laugh. "We have to talk first, Eden." He put her firmly away from him, standing up. "I want there to be no misunderstandings between us when I make you mine."

"But, Jason—"

"I know, darling." He bent to kiss her lightly on the lips, his caresses soothing her now, dulling her passions until he was ready to rekindle the flame. "But you have to listen to what I have to say."

"Yes, Jason."

"Behave!" he warned. "Now I'll deal with Isobel's accusation first."

"Which one?" Eden asked dryly.

"She said I wasn't in love with you, that I wanted to marry you only so that I could have complete control. She was wrong about both those things. I love you very much, very, very much. As for marrying you, I seem to remember I encouraged you to marry Tim when we first met, and later on, too. It was only when my own love for you became so strong that I couldn't bear the thought of another man near you that I knew I had to make you mine. But I tried to keep away from you, Eden. I tried because I knew exactly what you would think when you found out about that ridiculous condition in David's will. I would have tried to make him change his mind about that if I had known about it, but unfortunately it was too late, for him as well as for me. I think I fell in love with you on sight.''

"Oh, no, I'm sure you didn't," she laughed. "You despised me.''

"No, I wanted you. But it just wasn't right: David was my partner and you were his granddaughter.''

"Why was it no one ever mentioned that the two of you were partners?''

He shrugged. "Perhaps we all thought you knew. Anyway, it didn't seem that important, not until Isobel made it so. But that didn't really matter, none of it mattered. David was at the root of all the trouble. As soon as I had told you about that condition in the will you would have begun to suspect me—I knew that as soon as Isobel told you. So I promised you a year, a year during which you could marry someone else if you wanted to.''

Her eyes were wide. "But you never told me. You just let me go, let me think I would never see you again.''

"If I had told you it would have defeated the object. I arrived in the States yesterday. I met Claire for dinner, to talk business, nothing else," he told her firmly. "And today I telephoned you.''

"You...you called me?''

"The maid told me you were having dinner with a Mr. Channing this evening," he said with remembered bitterness. "And when I saw you, you said you were going to marry him. But are you sure about me now? If we get married you aren't going to throw the partnership in my face every time we argue?''

"Actually," she said softly, "I've thought of a good solution to that."

He raised his eyebrows. "You have?"

She snuggled against him, desire flaming between them again. "Mmm," she nodded. "An ideal solution, in fact."

"Well, don't keep me in suspense."

"Our son shall be the sole owner," she announced triumphantly.

"Our son...." Jason's eyes turned black, eyes she had once thought glacial, eyes that had suddenly melted. For her, only for her.

"Would you like that?" she smiled.

"As long as we can start work on our progeny right now. Tomorrow we can start making the arrangements for our wedding, but right now no more talking, hmm?" His lips probed her throat.

"No more talking," she confirmed. And there wasn't, not for a long time.